Non
call h
She g
After
decide
then
Usbor
writes
first, T
and longlisted for the Carnegie.

Find Non on Twitter (@NonPratt).

Other books by Non Pratt:

Trouble

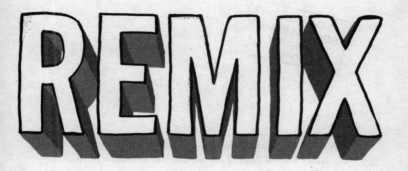

NON PRATT

WALKER
BOOKS

First published 2015 by Walker Books Ltd
87 Vauxhall Walk, London SE11 5HJ

2 4 6 8 10 9 7 5 3 1

Text © 2015 Leonie Parish
Cover illustration © 2015 Jimmy Turrell

This book has been typeset in Fairfield and Avenir

Printed and bound in Great Britain by Clays Ltd, St Ives plc

British Library Cataloguing in Publication Data:
a catalogue record for this book is available from the British Library

ISBN 978-1-4063-4770-8

www.walker.co.uk

For Lora,
my first – and best – festival buddy

FRIDAY

FRIDAY

KAZ

It's not unusual to wake up to at least two or three messages sent by my best friend during the hours all the normal people use for sleeping. Today there are fourteen.

Should I bother taking wellies with me? Sent at 00.23, which is *technically* the day that we're leaving for the festival. I'm not surprised – Ruby isn't so much last minute as last nanosecond.

Decided against wellies. They make you sweaty. Sweat foot vs trench foot.

Not that I'm hoping for trench foot. I just Googled it. Gross.

She's embellished this with a particularly helpful (disturbing) picture of a rotting foot.

Can't find my good bra. The purple one that fastens at the front and makes me look like I've got something inside. Did I leave it at yours last Friday?

Bra was in the laundry and smells of beer (???) now in the washing machine. Going to make a playlist for the journey while I wait for it to finish. Requests?

Sans helpful input from you, this playlist is 80% Gold'ntone. At this rate it'll be longer than their set on Saturday. (SATURDAY!!!)

Got distracted from making the playlist by Tumblring Wexler pics. Here's the best.

Adam Wexler, lead singer of Gold'ntone, smoulders from my phone as he pulls up the collar of an expensive-looking jacket. (It's a distinct improvement on the diseased foot.) His teeth bite down on his bottom lip as if suppressing a smile. I only have to speculate about what he's thinking for my breath to accelerate and my cheeks to burn.

Are your eyes totally having sex with that picture? Because mine are.

(Just my eyes.)

OVERSHARE KLAXON.

(Joking – I really am just looking at it with my eyes.)

God. You're so boring when you're asleep.

Needless to say, the call I make goes straight to voicemail.

"*Ruby here. Your call is very important to me, so please leave a message. Unless you are Stuart Cheating Shitbag Garside, in which case, fuck right off.*"

My name might not be Stuart Garside, but I decline to leave a message anyway since she never checks them. I write one instead.

My eyes thank you for the wake-up Wexler sex – it *almost* makes up for the fact that you'll have neglected to put any Little John songs on that playlist. (Please rectify.) Also, you seem confused about the smell of your bra. Maybe this photo will help.

Taken last week, it's of Ruby, standing on the dancefloor, arms wide, head thrown back, mouth open in an all-consuming laugh as an anonymous pair of arms showers her with a bottle of beer as if it's champagne.

Time to actually get out of bed.

The bathroom shows evidence of my sister – saturated bathmat, towels on the floor and an apothecary's worth of products surrounding the sink. She's used all the hot water too.

"Why do you smell like my new body oil?" Naomi asks when I come back after my shower. She is sitting in the middle of my bed, flipping through one of my magazines from which she's already ripped a pile of discount vouchers.

"Why are you in my room?" I ask. "Don't you have kittens to skin or dreams to crush? Some packing to finish?"

"It's finished. I've nothing to do until Dad gets here." (Except annoy me, obviously.)

Naomi blackmailed a weekend trip to London out of him when she found out he'd bought my Remix ticket. She doesn't seem to care that it was a reward for revising so hard for my exams, but then Naomi doesn't care about anything other than herself. My sister is two years younger and two hundred times more self-absorbed – a character trait I rely on when I pad over to where my clothes are hanging on the wardrobe door. I'd much rather she studied the outfits in that magazine than the one I'm about to put on…

"*That's* what you're wearing?" Naomi says, dashing my hopes. "Is it new?"

"Mm-hm." I bite my lips together as I pull the dress from the hanger, wishing she'd leave.

"And you're going to wear it to a scuzzy music festival?"

"Are you going to keep asking pointless questions?"

"Are you?" she whips back, but I'm too busy contorting myself into the dress to reply. When I turn round, Naomi's watching me with a supercilious smirk. She knows the reason why I'm making such an effort. Last week she told me that she'd found out my ex-boyfriend was going to Remix too. Tom's dad and ours have been friends since university and although Tom and I haven't been to each other's houses since the break-up, that hasn't stopped the dads. My sister overheard them grumbling about having to pay extortionate ticket prices over a late-night game of *Halo*. Since then she's been using this knowledge to her advantage. Naomi knows I'd rather cover all her chores than risk Mum – or Ruby – finding out about Tom going this weekend.

I meet her gaze in the mirror as I twist my hair to dry in better curls.

I don't trust the look on her face. "What?"

"Why so suspicious, Karizma?" Naomi is the sort of person who refuses to use nicknames. "I was just thinking you look almost decent."

"Let's hope Tom thinks so," I mutter. Although I'd rather he ranked me a little higher than "almost".

"Just don't ruin the effect by following him around with stupid puppy-dog eyes and agreeing with every little thing he says."

Naomi has officially exceeded her tolerance quota. "You can leave any second now."

Rolling her eyes, she collects the vouchers she's thieved from my magazine and stalks towards the door. "I'm only trying to help – although God knows why. You might be boring and your eyebrows need threading, but even you can do better than a tedious meathead with terrible trousers."

Naomi's never been Tom's biggest fan.

"At what point were you going to say something helpful?"

"Don't make yourself too available, Karizma. People work harder for the things they can't have."

"Exactly how many people have you been out with?"

She smiles, a tightening of the lips and an arch of well-threaded eyebrows. "No one's worked hard enough."

Honestly, I can't see why they'd want to.

RUBY

Putting your bra on to wash the night before you want to wear it is a pretty stupid idea. Not taking it out until the next morning is an even stupider one.

"What are you doing?" Lee is standing in the doorway of our parents' bedroom.

13

"Drying my bra," I shout back over the noise of the hairdryer. Even though I'm using my mother's super-powerful, super-posh one, it's taking ages. That's the problem with padding – it absorbs like a motherfucker.

"Ever heard of a tumble dryer?"

"You know nothing."

"About women's underwear? You're right. I don't." There's a pause. "Good job they've left for work already."

I don't have anything to say to that. Hairdryer aside, it's hard to feel any joy that my parents' idea of a decent goodbye is a Post-it note on my door.

Didn't want to wake you. Listen to Lee and do your best not to get into any trouble.

They didn't even sign off. Further proof that daughter/parental relations are at an all-time low.

Lee's still in the doorway, looking annoyingly like someone who's packed. Not much of a surprise since he's had to get ready to leave for Australia on Tuesday. Everything's in piles on his bedroom floor: "Stuff to Stay", "Stuff to Take Around the World", "Stuff to Take to Remix". My bedroom floor is covered in one big pile of "Stuff That Ruby Can't Be Arsed to Put Away". A category that includes all the things I was supposed to have packed last night before I got distracted with playlists and Wexler pics.

"How much do you love me?" I shout over the hairdryer.

"Enough to let you come to a music festival with me."

There's a time limit on how long he can milk that one, but it's best not to mention it when I'm fishing for a favour.

"Do you love me enough to let me come to a music festival with you *and* get me some breakfast whilst I finish packing?"

Apparently he does. By the time he returns, I'm in my room, the bra sufficiently dry for me to be wearing it under the Stiff Records T-shirt that violated St Felicity's School for Young Ladies' "code of conduct and civil decency" on mufti day. I made a point of wearing it to my last exam – just for good measure. Lee slides a plate of custard creams and a mug of black coffee into the space I've just cleared by elbowing some sketchbooks off my desk – my hands are kind of occupied, my fingers covered in eyeshadow because I can't find my brushes.

"You've always been my favourite," I say, blowing him a kiss in the mirror.

"Like that would be hard." Lee shifts some stuff off the end of my bed so he can sit down.

"Ed's in the running," I say. Mostly because Ed, who's so old now that he's got a job, a flat and a fiancée, used to let me stay up late and watch films with him whenever he was roped into babysitting. That backfired when *Terminator 2* gave me nightmares and our parents passed babysitting duties to Callum, who made every one of the four years he had on me count double by refusing to share snacks and forcing me to go to bed on time.

"You're right. Ed's top of my list, Callum next, *then* you," Lee says, grinning at me, and I stick my tongue out at the same time as I poke myself in the eye. I'm not great at multitasking.

Lee's lying anyway. I've lost count of the number of times we've agreed that this has been the best year of our lives now that Callum has taken his sarcasm and stupid speccy face off to university along with his back catalogue of *National Geographic* and foreign film boxsets.

Time to abort the make-up mission. I have a) run out of time and b) started to look as if I'd have been better off mashing my face into an eyeshadow palette and hoping for the best. Also c) Lee is eating my breakfast – something he is only too happy to demonstrate by opening his mouth to show me a half-chewed custard cream.

"You're disgusting. I don't know how Owen puts up with you." I shovel three biscuits in at once while Lee checks his phone.

"You can ask him yourself, since he's just pulled up." Lee looks at the rucksack on my bed. It's so empty that it's folded in on itself like a mouth without teeth. "Get a shift on, Pubes, or I'll leave you behind."

"Always abandoning me," I mutter, but Lee shoots me a look that kills the joke dead. Guess now's not the time to guilt-trip him about his gap year – the closer next Tuesday gets, the touchier he's become.

Whatever. I've a festival to pack for.

When Lee shouts up that they're ready to go, I'm already out of the bedroom door, fully loaded with rucksack, sleeping bag and a pocketful of custard creams. Mostly charged phone in hand, I dial Kaz.

"Be ready, my friend. We're coming to—"

"Did you put any Little John on the playlist?"

"Don't interrupt. I was trying to be all cool and movie-like," I say, hurrying down the stairs.

"I'm sorry, please go ahead."

"Be ready, my friend. We're coming to get you. The weekend officially starts *now*."

There's a pause. "You've forgotten to put any Little John songs on the playlist, haven't you?"

"Yes."

2 • BRING ON THE WORLD

RUBY

I bounce into the front seat next to Owen and give him a kiss on the cheek that nearly knocks the sunnies from his face.

"Did anyone ever tell you that you were the best?" I say by way of greeting.

"No. They did not."

"Liar." Lee climbs up next to me. "I tell you that all the time."

Given that my brother usually expresses love via the medium of piss-taking I'm not surprised that his boyfriend responds with a deeply sceptical silence. "Well, *I'm* telling you anyway. You" – I poke Owen in the fattest part of his arm, but he still winces, the wimp – "are the best."

"Someone's in a good mood." Owen grins, coaxing his ancient van into life.

Lee leans round me and stage-whispers, *"It's not too late to leave her at home."*

I poke him in the arm too, in the sweet spot right below what passes for a bicep on his skinny-ass body. "Shut up, Wee."

"Poo-by." Lee tries to squash me against Owen, who gently pushes me away and says something about "Not when I'm driving".

The second we turn onto the seafront we hit traffic, Clifton's clock tower looming over us in case we'd forgotten that we were already running late. Before anyone can point out that this is my fault, I hook up my phone and whack the stereo on. The first track on my playlist opens with an *immense* riff that earns me a fierce nod of approval from the chauffeur and a threat to throw me out on the tarmac from Lee, who's never had the best taste in music.

When I remind him that he's only got himself to blame for bringing me along, he's forced to agree, although his eyes are smiling as much as mine when he says it.

Two weeks after I'd dumped Stu I was in the middle of watching *Harry Potter and the Half-Blood Prince* in my room when Lee knocked on the door and clocked the giant bowl of popcorn, half-empty bottle of Coke and freeze-frame of Ron and Hermione.

"Good to see I'm not interrupting anything."

I made room for him on the bed and pressed play. All of us have radically different taste in films: Lee likes fantasy, Ed likes action and Callum likes anything wanky. I like animation. Harry Potter's the only franchise we agree on – if it weren't for that, Christmas TV viewing chez Kalinski would be a bloodbath.

Lee took a handful of popcorn and tried to throw it into his mouth.

"You're getting popcorn in my bed."

"You can snack on it later."

"Mmm. Stale bed-popcorn. My favourite."

"How many times have you watched these films in the last two weeks, Rubert?"

I took a swig of Coke instead of replying.

"Because it's pretty unhealthy to spend every waking second wondering what house you'd be in—"

"Gryffindor." Lee would be Ravenclaw, Callum Slytherin, Ed Hufflepuff. We're not one of those magical families that belong in the same Hogwarts house. We're not even one of those non-magical families that belong in the same *actual* house.

"—or what subject you'd be best at."

"Care of Magical Creatures." The Buzzfeed quiz I did got that wrong – like *I'd* be any good at Potions.

"Ruby." When Lee real-names me, it means he's serious. He stopped the film and turned to look at me. "Are you all right?"

"I'm sick of people asking me that. I'm fine. I'm just pissed off and bored and" – I shrugged – "I don't know what to do with myself with Kaz in Germany and everyone else on holiday or on work placements or whatever."

Truth was that I didn't much feel like hanging out with anyone other than Kaz, who was away on a choir tour. Our other friends kept looking at me like I'd just lost *The X Factor* final or something, when all I'd done was lose a boyfriend. And *I* was the one who did the losing. Très irritating. I am nobody's victim.

"How about we make a deal?" Lee said.

I wasn't sure where he was going with this.

"There's some late shifts free at the ice-cream place…"

I pulled a face. I already had a Saturday job that sucked down at The Rock Shop, selling sweets to tourists with more money than sense. Summer season in a small seaside town might pay well, but it's tedium squared.

"It's money you could put to good use."

"What sort of use?"

"Like paying me back if I bought you a weekend ticket to Remix."

Was he serious? He certainly looked it, only…

"You think the parentals would actually let me go?" My parents had stopped me from going to see Owen's band Hydro because it was on a school night *during study leave*.

"You forget I can be more persuasive than you. This'll be my last chance to hang out with you before I go away and you could *really* do with cheering up." Lee put on his best Very Responsible Face and laid his hand on his heart. "Plus I swear on my duties as a brother to supervise you – and perhaps your good friend Kaz?"

"Seriously, you'd do that? Persuade them to let me go *and* let me and Kaz camp with you?"

This was an even bigger deal than it sounded, since Lee wasn't going with the usual suspects from Dukes, but Owen and his mates from the cool college. People I'd actually *like* hanging out with for a weekend.

"Only if you stop spending all your time at Hogwarts and start doing something useful, like selling every-flavour ice cream to Muggles."

Which is exactly what I did.

Dad picked Naomi up half an hour ago and the house is quiet but for the clicking of keys coming from the front room, where I find Mum, sitting on the sofa, surrounded by a sea of paper. I perch on the arm, since the space next to her is occupied by the cat. Everyone in this house knows better than to disturb Morag.

"What are you doing?" I ask.

"Expenses." As far as I can work out, being a publicist is nothing *but* expenses – and possibly publicizing things, although I see less of that around the house. "With you and Naomi out of the way I'll have everything done by the time I go back to work on Tuesday." Mum glances up from her laptop and smiles.

I'm sure she's only trying to make me feel better – Mum and Dad divide bank holidays between them and this one was meant to be hers until my Remix request disrupted the system.

"There's cassoulet in the freezer and I've saved Wok This Way's number on to the phone. You like Number Forty-two with special fried rice, no prawns," I say, repeating what I've written on the kitchen whiteboard.

"Aren't mothers supposed to worry about daughters?"

"We all know I'm the responsible one." Because I am.

"Speaking of which, did you pack those condoms I left on your bed?"

"Yes. Thanks for those." I can feel myself burning up – I thought I'd dodged that conversational bullet.

Mum doesn't look up from her spreadsheet as she embellishes on her choice of prophylactic. "They're the featherlight ones that feel like the real thing, so there's no excuse not to wear one."

I really wish she'd stop talking. Or that the others would get here. Or that my top lip would produce so much sweat that I'll drown in my own perspiration.

Sensing my discomfort, Mum slides the computer off her lap so she can shuffle closer and rest a reassuring hand on my knee. "I've been to festivals" – which is news to me – "I know what it's like. Two gorgeous girls and a field full of boys—"

"You make it sound like we're harvesting them."

"I just don't want you to cut yourself when you swing the scythe."

"Now it sounds like we're planning to kill them."

Mum smiles as she reaches up to stroke the hair back off my face, twisting a curl around her finger before letting it ping back. "Just be safe, chicken. That's all."

If she knew the only person I wanted to play it safe with was my ex-boyfriend, this would be a very different conversation.

3 • THINKING ABOUT YOU

KAZ

Two hours later and Owen eventually pulls up at the end of a row of cars in a field that passes for a car park. Although the campsite and arena are hidden by a dip in the land, there's no mistaking which way we'll find them as torrents of festival-goers flow towards a dirt track lined with tents where staff exchange tickets for wristbands.

Ruby is beside herself with excitement. Her adrenalin levels increased exponentially with every junction we passed on the motorway and she can barely stand still, despite the rucksack on her back and the crate of supplies Lee's told her she has to carry part of the way. It is impossible to hold a conversation with her as her attention ricochets from tour T-shirts to tattoos to hot boys in sunglasses to girls with cool hair.

Now is definitely not the time to tell her about Tom.

As we shuffle forwards in the crush, I scan the crowd around me – boys who've taken off their tops and tucked them into the back of their shorts, girls in bikini tops and shorts so short they're practically thongs, middle-aged rockers whose tattoos have grown blurred with age. I catch sight of a boy in the crowd who sends a smile in my direction. I glance away before it arrives.

He isn't the one I was looking for.

RUBY

We've found a tidy little spot halfway up the field marked SOUTH SLOPE. Our tent is up in record time, and I leave Kaz to unpack and go to offer my services to Lee and Owen. They're wrestling with the canvas monstrosity that me and my brothers used to cram into when holidays were compromised by four sets of school fees. There's only one set left now … or none at all, given the massive question mark over whether Flickers will have me back after the results I got.

"Need any help?" I offer, just as one of the poles slips and cracks Lee across the knuckles. He gives me a murderous look, which I take as instruction to go back where I came from – i.e. the tent, where Kaz is *still* unpacking. Admittedly I cheated by not packing properly in the first place, but it looks as if Kaz has brought her entire wardrobe.

"You know we're only here three nights, right?"

Kaz gives me Unimpressed Face. "It's called being prepared."

"What, for a Who Has the Most Tea Dresses Competition?" Kaz throws a ball of thermal socks at my face and I start rooting around in her toiletries bag.

"What are you doing?" Kaz is refolding her pyjamas to put in her sleeping bag. I have not brought any pyjamas. Or any deodorant. Or toothpaste.

"Looking for deodorant. And toothpaste." But that's not what I find. "Oh my God, Karizma Asante-Blake –

have you come prepared for an *orgy*?"

Kaz looks very hot and bothered and actually drops the shirt she's trying to fold as I brandish the MASSIVE box of condoms I've just discovered.

"Mum gave them to me."

"And she thinks *you're* going to need all these?" The packet says TWENTY-FOUR. Kaz hasn't even had sex with *one* person yet – her and Tom went out for nine months and didn't manage to get round to getting it on. One weekend's barely going to be enough for her to *look* at another boy, let alone boff one.

"You know what my mum's like," Kaz says.

I do. Afua's well cool. Not like my mum, who had a shit fit when she found a blister pack of the pill under my pillow and banned me from seeing Stu for a fortnight. She'd have banned me for life if she could.

"Still, your mum's right to be worried, dude." I eye her outfit. "The way you look in that dress this weekend will be like a gender-flipped Lynx ad."

It's not an outfit I've seen before and Kaz is showing a lot more off than she's usually comfortable with. I thoroughly approve.

KAZ

It's the first time Ruby's mentioned my dress and now would be the perfect time to tell her why I'm wearing it.

What I actually say is, "I'm sure I'll be beating them off with a stick."

"You know *beating them off* usually works best with your hand?" Ruby's doubled over, laughing so much at her own innuendo that the second ball of socks I throw at her misses. Once she's recovered, she rips off a strip of condoms and tucks it into her pocket before declaring that I have finished unpacking (I haven't) and crawling out of the tent. Where Ruby leads, I follow. Even if I haven't finished unpacking.

RUBY

Instead of heading down to the bottom of the hill where there's a cluster of fair rides and a ton of people who've yet to find a place to pitch their tent, we walk up to the line of stalls at the top. Almost immediately I'm distracted by one that's full to brimming with the most tasteless tat I've ever seen. Within a minute of dragging Kaz inside, I strike gold in the form of an awesome penis-shaped bong.

"Oh God, do you have to?" Kaz says as I make her hold it so I can take a photo that I send to Ed asking him if he needs a flat-warming present – although since Emma made him get rid of his old lava lamp, I'm not sure she'll go for the purple-penis bong.

"Yes, I absolutely do. It is perfection in glass form." I take it from her to hold it close to my face and stroke it lovingly as Kaz turns away, hissing at me to put it down.

Her advice comes too late. Someone, namely the stallholder, has noticed. "Buying for yourself or a friend?"

I glance round to see if there's any further opportunity to humiliate Kaz, but she's disowned me and is trying to look *extremely* interested in the racks of novelty socks outside.

"Much as I love an anatomically accurate appendage," – I glance at the stallholder again, he's quite cute – "I think I'm going to pass on this particular occasion."

"You sure? I'll do you a *dicks*-count." His eyes twinkle as I shake my head and smile.

"How long's that one been *cum*-ing?" I shoot back and this time he's the one laughing. Again with the quite cute.

"I'm *glans* you asked?" He's screwing up his face in anticipation of my scorn. To be fair, he deserves it for that one.

"I'm all out of penis puns, I'm afraid," I say, ignoring the buzz my phone makes with Ed's reply. I'm just getting into my groove here.

KAZ

My best friend and I are very different when it comes to boys. Ruby adopts a scattergun approach of flirting with anyone she sees regardless of sensible limiting factors such as (in the stallholder's case) age. Whereas I can only flirt with someone I actually fancy, which is unfortunate since there is only one person I know who meets that criteria.

When we booked the Remix tickets, Ruby made it clear that hot boys were part of the plan – and not just for her. It was only a month after things had ended with Tom and even though I wasn't wildly enthusiastic about the idea of looking for someone new, Ruby assumed I'd be over him by now and ready for action.

Only I'm not. It hasn't been as easy for me to recover from Tom as it has been for Ruby and Stu. Tom wasn't just my first boyfriend, he was the first boy I ever fancied – when I was ten and saw him in cricket whites. Tom was my first crush, my first kiss, my first love… He was supposed to be my *first*. It's hard to look at other boys and see someone I might Do It with when I've always assumed that person was going to be Tom.

I really need to tell Ruby about him being here.

RUBY

Kaz does not seem especially interested in my assessment of Cute Stallholder Guy.

"Does he have a name?" Kaz cuts through what I was saying.

"I assume so." I glance back at the stall thoughtfully. "Maybe I'll find out later…"

It's meant to be a joke – the guy was good for a warm-up flirt, not actual gameplay – but Kaz is giving me the same look she's been giving me all summer, the one that screams, "I think you're a depraved sexpot."

I'm not so much a depraved sexpot as a deprived one. I've not had any since Stu, which is kind of like having champagne on tap one minute and going cold turkey the next. Well, not *cold* cold turkey. Lukewarm turkey. I've still got my right hand and an overactive imagination –

although there's only so far that a certain expertise and an Adam Wexler fantasy can take me. It doesn't matter if those fantasies have gone all the way and then some, I'm someone who likes the feel of another body on mine, skin on skin, lips and tongues and teeth. The warmth, the smell, the taste.

"Can we go and sit somewhere for a bit?" Kaz says out of the blue, which I'm grateful for. I don't actually want Stu in my head when I've left Clifton to get away from him.

Kaz is fiddling with her pendant, so I figure there's something she wants to talk about. Something I won't like… We find a shady spot under some trees since the sun is trying to BURN THE FLESH FROM MY BONES and I clamber to sit on the fence so I'm eye level with the necklace-twiddling nutter in front of me.

"What's up?" I ask.

KAZ

Best to treat this like a plaster and rip it off in three … two … one…

"Tom's here."

"You what?" Ruby actually glances over her shoulder as if he's materialized behind her. "Tom's where?"

"Here. At Remix."

"O…K…" Ruby looks entirely nonplussed. "And this is the first I'm hearing of it because?"

But I don't have to say anything for her to know the answer.

I am such a wimp sometimes.

RUBY

Brilliant.

Thomas sodding Selkirk.

Kaz is gabbling about how she only found out the other day and she wasn't sure whether to even mention it because we're probably not going to bump into him anyway when there are so many people here.

It's all just noise to cover up what she really wants to happen: she wants to see Tom. All summer – ever since they split – by so many twists of fate that it's been a cat's cradle of coincidence, Tom and Kaz have failed to bump into each other. She was on choir tour, he went away with his family to France, Kaz got shipped off to Wales. In the week and a half in which they've both been within sight of the sea, they've not been within sight of each other.

There's no point fighting it. Much as I want Kaz to get on with her life and into someone else's pants, it's not going to happen if she's on red alert for her ex.

So much for leaving all that shit behind.

KAZ

Ruby stops me with a resigned wave of her hand. "I think we should just go find him. Get it over with."

My response to this is to throw my arms around her waist and lift her from the fence, my cheeks hurting from grinning a wide and incredulous grin.

"Are you sure?" I drop her unceremoniously on the floor.

"I suppose." She squints against the sun behind me. "But don't pull that shit again, you hear? This is you and me – we don't do secrets." There's a moment in which she watches me before her expression relaxes. "Now. Fire your special flare gun that forms an image of a man wearing slightly too-short trousers, light a candle and sing 'Jerusalem' backwards or whatever. Summon the Selkirk."

I hold up my phone with Tom's number on the screen. "Or I could just use this, like a normal person."

He answers on the second ring.

"Hey, Tom," I say, doing an excellent impression of Mickey Mouse.

"You called, m'dear?" The friendliness of his voice – the familiarity – renders me mute for a moment. "Hello, Kaz…?"

"Sorry, yes, hi. Umm… I heard you'd be here as well. From Naomi. Or Dad. No – Naomi!" Either way it sounds like I've been keeping tabs on him. "Dad's taking Naomi to London." *Stop talking now, mouth.* "For the weekend. Naomi said that your dad said—"

Ruby actually leaps forward and puts both hands over my mouth, whispering, *"Shut. Up."*

Tom doesn't seem to mind that I ended my last sentence with a "whumph", but I can hear the smile in his voice when he says, "If by 'here' you mean Remix, then yes. We just got here. Me and Naj and Roly."

Now what?

Ruby, whose eyeballs have been rolling around so much I'm surprised they're still in the sockets, mutters,

"For fuck's sake" and takes my phone. "Hey, Tom, how's it going? We're in the middle of exploring the campsite and wondered whether we should come and explore your part of it, wherever that may be. Possibly explore whatever food you've got. And whatever drinks."

There's a pause. "Totally like scavengers. Think of us as a particularly sexy pair of racoons."

I can hear him laughing from here, no more immune to the Ruby Effect than anyone else. She concentrates as he explains where they are.

"Got it. See you in five." Handing me the phone back, Ruby looks at me for a long moment. "Are you *sure* about this, Kaz?"

4 • NOT MY IDEA

KAZ

All the way from South Slope to where Tom's camped in Three-Tree Field I tell myself the same thing.

I am sure. I am sure. I am sure.

Once I've seen Tom we can get on with our weekend. It won't change anything. I just want to say hi, to show how fine I am being friends. Just to prove it to myself – to Tom – to Ruby. Just to double-check that's all we are. It's been a long time and maybe Tom's missed me the way I have him…

Tom told Ruby that they're camped next to someone flying a fluorescent pink Jolly Roger. Ruby spots the flag first. I spot the boy.

Tom looks the way I always imagine him. Body broad enough to hold me, tall enough to make me safe – big but gentle, like a bear from a fairy tale or a picture book. His haircut is the same one he's always had (apart from the winter of the unwise buzzcut) and the smile he's wearing as he talks to the person next to him is the smile I've missed every second of the last sixty-nine days, twenty-two hours and … twenty-three minutes.

Maybe I am not so sure about this after all.

RUBY

How can Kaz fancy someone with such appalling trousers?

Oblivious to the awkward, Tom gives Kaz a hug before turning to me as I take a quick step back and nearly stack it on a guy rope. I can fake friendly on a phone call, but Tom is not a person I am prepared to hug. Which definitely puts him in the minority, because I am usually all about the hugs.

"Hello, Tom," I say.

There's a moment in which Tom and I communicate our feelings without having to say a word. He knows that I would quite happily strangle him with the rogue guy rope I've just dislodged and I know that he doesn't think he deserves it.

Tom Selkirk buys into his own reputation as a nice guy. One who helps little old ladies with their shopping and gives up his seat on the bus to pregnant women. A reputation that isn't a reality.

Tom has known Kaz longer than I have – they spent summers together, shared hiding places and secrets and sweets and a healthy resentment of Naomi. They have the kind of history that should have been worth more than an evening's conversation and the eternally shit sentence "I just don't see you like that any more."

When I am wizened and old and have forgotten how to use a hairbrush, I'll still remember the look on my best mate's face as I sat on the sofa with her that same night, and the tears she couldn't stop as she endlessly,

endlessly asked me what was wrong with her. The answer is nothing. She is Kaz. She is *perfect* – and this boy, this normal, "nice" boy, who was meant to be as much friend as boyfriend, made her feel worthless.

Tell me how I'm ever supposed to forgive that.

KAZ

Tom introduces me to the three girls from the camp next to theirs (the one with the Jolly Roger) and the girls make polite noises, whilst looking not entirely happy to have Ruby bowl up and sit down between Roly and Naj and take a handful of crisps from the bag Naj has just opened. Tom and his friends might be the year above us at Canterbury College, but Ruby's as comfortable in their company as if she was sitting with girls she sees every day at Flickers.

"So how've you been?" Tom passes me a coffee brewed on their gas stove. I like that it's exactly the way I take it without me having to ask.

"Fine." I smile at the surface of my drink, thinking how peculiar it is to be seeing him for the first time in a field a hundred miles from the town where we both live. "How was France?" Every year Tom and his cousins stay with his grandparents in Brittany. This year I was supposed to go too.

"Bof," Tom says, before changing the subject. "Speaking of French, Dad said you got a set of insanely good results?"

"I did better than I expected."

"Some of us always knew you were a genius," he says.

I elbow him in the side and he bumps me back. It feels nice. "What about Ruby?"

I look over to where Ruby is sitting, trying (failing) to hide how much she wants to leave.

It would feel wrong to talk about it to anyone else. But this is Tom. "Not brilliantly. Not well enough."

He knows what I mean, and I can feel him looking at me as I look at Ruby. She's been my best friend since I started at Flickers in Year 7 – even if she's there to resit, she won't be in any of my classes, she won't be sitting in the common room in the sixth-form block, wearing her own clothes, but back in the school, forced into a uniform that she couldn't wait to get out of.

Or there's the other option that neither of us have talked about – that Ruby won't be at Flickers at all.

I can be Kaz without Tom if I have to. I don't know whether I can be Kaz without Ruby.

RUBY

I message Lee.

Oh my God, I'm so bored.

His reply: *Ungrateful much? I buy you a ticket, sort out your ride, buy your booze...*

I'm paying you back for all those things. Anyway, that was supposed to be a HINT FOR YOU TO RING ME. I need an excuse here.

Turning the volume up, I put my phone down and wait.

The girl next to Roly titters and twirls a strand of her

hair round like a little helicopter – I'm sure she thinks she looks cute. She looks like an idiot. Not that Roly seems to mind.

I'm still waiting…

Naj shakes a fresh bag of crisps at me – an act that irritates one of the other girls next to him, who I think must fancy him, judging by the death glares she's been giving me.

Waiting…

I don't want to commit to more crisps and that girl is welcome to—

Finally my phone blares out Lee's signature *Game of Thrones* theme tune and I stand up to answer it.

"THERE'S NO PLACE LIKE HOME," Lee bellows into my ear. "Get your ass back here, Ruby Slipper." And then he hangs up.

"OK." I smile, pretending he's still there. "Will do." Then I look up at my audience. "That was my brother. I've got to go."

Kaz hasn't even noticed I've stood up, and when I call out her name, she looks dazed and confused, as if she's surprised to find I'm here at all.

"You coming?" I ask, watching the panic of indecision in her eyes: piss me off or deny herself some bonus Tom time?

"Five minutes?" Kaz looks hopeful, but when she says minutes she means hours, and there's no way I can manage that long with only Tom's friends and the girls who want to pull them for company. I don't want to leave

Kaz here either, but if I make a fuss, I'll be acting all ogre-ish, which is apparently something I do and I am *not* prepared to be the bad guy here.

"Lee wants me for something" – which is the lamest of all the lies – "so I'll head off now. See you when you're done?"

KAZ

Ruby waves goodbye with one hand, but I see her curl the index finger of the other into a hook against her thigh. It's a signal I'm more used to giving than receiving – *you have half an hour before I try to find you*. Back when we went to The Cellar, before Ruby declared it a no-fly zone after she broke up with Stu, I'd find him and Ruby half an hour before the last bus home to Mum's and give the sign before I rejoined everyone else on the dancefloor. It feels strange for Ruby to be using it on me and Tom.

Tom is sitting so close that his elbow brushes my side as he reaches to catch a bag of crisps. When he leans back to open them, I catch a faint hint of the Tom-smell I've been yearning for all summer. Suddenly half an hour doesn't seem very long at all, but Ruby's too far away now for me to call her back.

RUBY

There's supposed to be some kind of rivalry between Clifton's nearest private schools (Flickers and Dukes) and the massive comprehensive (Canterbury), only it's not something you ever see off the hockey/football/rugby pitch. We're all too busy trying to get off with each other. Clifton is a small town with a high percentage of horny teenagers and we can't afford to limit ourselves – just as well, since Kaz went for Tom and both me and my brother went for what were upper-sixth Canterbury boys. Obviously Lee picked the most wisely. Not only is Owen the loveliest, he comes complete with a pretty cool set of friends.

"Ruby!" Anna gives me an enthusiastic hug. We've only seen each other a couple of times at Hydro gigs when we've both been showing Owen some support in the form of overly loud cheering and wolf-whistling, but Anna is easy to warm to. She gives me a squeeze and points to a large blue tent squashed up against ours. "Sorry we're camping on top of you, but Dongle refused to move his tent over."

The only two things I know about Dongle are that he once ate a Granny Smith apple by putting the whole thing in his mouth and he has a bit of a way with the ladies, so mostly I'm just relieved it's not his tent that's next to us. I can do without an audio sex show six inches from my head at two in the morning.

"Where's Lee?" I ask. Owen's artistically laying a ring of stones around some logs in the middle of the camp, but there's no sign of my brother.

"He and Parvati went to the festival shop," Anna says. "They went for extra firewood and emergency meat supplies, *because some idiot can't read a shopping list*."

Dongle, who has just emerged from his tent, looks over and grins. "Don't be so hard on yourself, Anna."

"I was being hard on *you*." Anna gives him a good-natured glare from under her fringe, but Dongle's attention sharpens on me.

"Hello. Do I know you?" The way his eyes twinkle – like he's good for a laugh – makes it easy to believe what Lee's told me about the girls. No idea about the apple thing. That kind of shit I've got to see to believe.

"Not yet." I grin. "Ruby. Nice to meet you."

"Dave. Call me Dongle." We shake hands and Anna turns round to grab one of the camping chairs they've brought, displaying the waistband of a pair of pants that reads TUESDAY. There is a lot I like about Anna.

The three of us sit in a line to catch the best of the sun, Owen at our feet, still perfecting his pyre. Anna reminds him it can't be too big or it'll get classified as a bonfire and get us thrown out.

"Only if he gets round to actually lighting it," Dongle says, receiving a back-handed slap to the shin from Owen.

Ignoring them, Anna asks where I've been.

"We bumped into some other Clifton people."

Owen glances up a little too quickly, but the match he's holding burns out to his fingers and he winces, distracted from our conversation again.

"Anyone we know?" Anna says, opening the cool box and handing me a beer without even hesitating before she passes another to Dongle and cracks one open for herself.

Owen's looking up from the fire again and it's clear he's interested in the answer.

"Tom Selkirk and his mates." At the sound of Tom's name, Owen seems to relax. "You might know them. They're the year below you guys?"

"Rugby Tom?" Dongle perks up and I nod. "He's a good guy. I like him." I stay quiet and sip my beer. "We should ask them over later."

Dongle doesn't catch my reaction to this suggestion, but Anna's faster.

"What and share our beer with strangers? I don't think so." She leans over and bumps her can to mine and winks. "Let's keep tonight simple, shall we?"

As I said, there's a lot I like about Anna.

KAZ

Is Tom flirting with me? I can feel him looking at me when I talk across the camp to Naj and Roly, and much as I'm trying to talk myself out of believing it, it certainly *feels* like there's something going on beneath the surface.

But even as I'm trying to work out how I can find an excuse to spend a little more time with him, my phone buzzes. Prepared to be annoyed with Ruby for hassling me ten minutes before she needs to, I discover it's from Mum.

Fuses gone. Help.

I wish my mother would take the step from "not needing a man" to "actually learning how to do things" instead of relying on me all the time. It's been five years since she left Dad and you'd have thought she might have discovered how to reset the fuse box by now.

"Mum needs me," I say to Tom. "She's tripped a fuse."

It might not be rocket science, but this isn't something I can do via text.

Reluctant to leave, I permit myself a quick hug goodbye, Naomi's *people work harder for the things they can't have* mantra preventing me from drawing a map to our camp and inviting Tom to the barbecue Lee promised we'd have when Owen's friends arrived.

"I'll see you later," I say, letting go.

"You will." This promise strikes a note of hope in my heart that tingles out through the whole of my body, and when I wave goodbye to the others, I'm *sure* I'm not imagining the sly look that passes between Roly and Naj.

I've reached the path by the time Mum answers my call.

"What were you doing, anyway?" I ask once I've explained how to solve the problem. "I thought this weekend was all about expenses."

"Morag knocked my water all over the extension lead. I'm taking this as a sign to give up work and start getting ready. Where's your red clutch bag?"

"Second drawer down. Hot date?"

"I certainly hope so. Want me to send a picture?"

"Immediately!"

"Hang up then."

When the picture comes through I text my approval. *Very respectable. I hope his intentions are as honourable as his appearance.*

Seconds later: *I hope they aren't.*

Should have kept some of those condoms aside for yourself.

It was buy one get one half price.

This makes me laugh so much that I don't look where I'm going and I walk smack into the back of a boy.

RUBY

The alarm on my phone goes. Kaz's half-hour is up.

KAZ

No. This is not right. This is very definitely *not* the ex that's supposed to be here.

Every town, even one as small and boring as Clifton-on-Sea, has a Stuart Garside. Someone with a reputation and an ego to match, he's a Google-Image definition of "bad boy": a hint of muscle under his vest; tattoo emerging from over his shoulder, curling round his bicep. He's not objectively beautiful – if you drew a picture of him (well, if Ruby did, since my attempt would be a stick man with eyebrows and a lip piercing) then you wouldn't think much of him. But a picture is not the same as a person.

Stu is *hot* … and the only way I'd touch him would be with a cattle prod. Or a Taser.

"Hello, Kaz." Stu's mouth curls into a slow, lazy smile of recognition. It's not the reaction I'd expect. Last time we spoke I was confronting him about the rumour he'd cheated on my best friend.

I'm so discombobulated that I hadn't even noticed my phone's going.

Stu nods at my left hand. "You going to answer that?"

I most certainly am not. "Dancing Queen" means it's Ruby (because she hates it – she set "Sweet Caroline" as mine in revenge). I hit reject without looking and a second later it buzzes her message.

"Hello, Stu," I finally manage.

The girl he's with (who I didn't register until now) looks from me to Stu. "Aren't you going to introduce us?"

Stu raises his eyebrows. "Now why would I do that?"

Before I can reassure her that it's not necessary, because I'm leaving, he's murmuring something to her, brushing her arm before she leaves.

Too late I realize that I missed my chance to do the same.

"It's been a while," he says, turning back to me.

"Not long enough."

This elicits a huff of laughter. "Anyone ever tell you that

grudges are unflattering?" There's a pause before he adds, "Nice dress though."

My immediate inclination is to thank him for the compliment, but I'll choke on the words before I say anything even remotely polite to him.

"So where is she, then?" Stu glances round then back at me, the silver stud of his labret piercing glinting as he moves.

"Where's who?" Even I think I sound stupid.

"You know I mean Ruby."

"Why are you asking?"

"You really are determined to make me work for this, aren't you?" I don't want Stu to work for anything. I want him to give up and crawl back to whoever's bed he just left. "I'm asking where Ruby is because she's your best friend. If you're here, then so is she. Somewhere." He looks thoughtful. "It'd be nice to say hi."

"No, it wouldn't."

"Ruby not over me, then?" The way his grin intensifies annoys me.

"Stay away from her, Stu."

"Is this you *looking out* for her again?" There's a flash of steel in his voice as he says it, echoing the phrase I used when I said he owed Ruby the truth about what he'd done.

"Perhaps if you hadn't cheated on my best friend in front of half of Clifton, I wouldn't need to."

"You saying I should have cheated in private?"

Stu makes me stupid. Even girls at The Cellar – prettier, more confident ones, more proficient in the art of attracting men – are reduced to giggling idiots when they try and talk to him. Not Ruby. *Never* Ruby. Flirt for flirt, she played him the same way he tried to play her – and she won.

For five months, Stuart Garside only had eyes for my best friend and from first kiss to last, he made her shine. She did the same for him … until he ruined it the way everyone, even Ruby, knew he would.

My phone buzzes yet another message and I glance down.

You rejected my call! Consider me outraged.

(That last message was a hint for you to call me back, btw.)

(As was that one.)

I feel you're missing the point. Call me back, dude. Your half-hour is up and I'm checking you're OK. xxx

I look up at Stu. "I'm going now."

"That's a shame. We were getting along so well." He's reverted to cocky once more. "We should do this again sometime."

"No, we shouldn't." I'm walking away, but Stu's keeping pace, his gait as effortless as his smile. "What are you doing?" I ask.

"Walking back to camp, like a good boy."

I stop. "You're not walking back to ours."

Stu stops too. We're the same height, but Stu has the kind of ego that strips mine bare and I feel smaller with every passing second.

"I'm walking back to *mine*," he says, stepping even closer to point over my shoulder before adding, "Unless you're inviting me to pay a visit?"

Stu considers my silence and my crossed arms, before giving a rueful shrug and starting up the hill.

"Don't even think about looking for her, Stu," I warn.

He half-turns, still walking, and calls back, "Telling me what to do, telling me what to think. Do you honestly believe you have any right to tell me *anything*, Kaz?"

6 • DIRTY LITTLE SECRET

RUBY

Lee and Parvati get back before Kaz does – although she did send me a suitably profuse apology with lots of kisses and emojis and a picture of a humble-looking bear.

I receive a hug that's more for show than for real from Parvati. From the super-mussed pixie crop to her Pantone-paint-chart nail varnish and the ironic way she's styled her Celine Dion T-shirt, everything about Parvati is measured, the way everything about Anna isn't.

Lee ignores me and drops an extra bag of firewood into Owen's lap.

"Not helpful, Lee." Owen hands the bag back, looking the closest to annoyed that I've ever seen him. Obviously the uncooperative fire is starting to get to him.

"I see that buying an extra bag of festival-endorsed and extortionately expensive firewood was a little bit premature." Lee nudges one of the unlit logs with his toe. "You planning on lighting this fire any time today, O?"

"It's harder than it looks." Owen's definitely getting tetchy.

"Did you not think these might help?" Lee pulls a box out of their tent and moves his finger along the letters as he reads, "*Firelighters*. And, look, there's a pretty picture of some flames."

Lee hands the box over with a grin as Parvati reaches up for a high five.

"Burn!" She slaps his palm.

"Or not-burn as the case may be." Lee laughs and reaches out to ruffle Owen's hair – a gesture Owen thwarts by ducking away, still looking pissed. Lee ignores him and opens the cool box. He goes for one of the revolting canned cocktails and then hands beers to Anna, Parvati and Dongle. When I reach for one, Lee gives me a look.

"Pace yourself, Puberty."

Ignoring him, I get my own beer. This is not the sort of thing I have ever listened to *any* of my brothers about, least of all this one.

"Where's Kaz?" Lee asks.

Dongle's keen to prove he's been paying attention. "With Rugby Tom."

"Selkirk? Bet that was cosy."

"That's one word for it," I mutter low enough that Dongle can't hear. Lee knows the way I feel about the Kaz/Tom situation.

"I feel like I'm missing something," Parvati pipes up from the rug, one arm draped artfully over her knees as she sits and sips her beer. "You're all talking in code. Rugby Tom, Kaz, who are these people?"

"Kaz is Ruby's friend who's camping with us," Owen says, finally emerging from his sulk as the firelighters glimmer beneath the logs. "Tom's her boyfriend—"

"*Ex*-boyfriend," Lee and I correct him at the same time.

"Right," Dongle says. "Tom's going out with that fit girl from the tearooms, isn't he?"

The way he says it, Dongle clearly thinks this is something we already know.

It most certainly is not.

KAZ

What am I supposed to do now? Do I tell Ruby that I've seen Stu – or will that spoil things for her? Will she become like I was when I was on the alert for Tom? Will every tattooed arm, every lean torso, every word that rhymes with "Stu" set her off? Only *worse* because I actually wanted to see Tom? From the second she ended things, Ruby could not have been clearer how she felt.

"It's over," she told me on the phone after she'd seen him. "Stu had sex with another girl at that house party."

"I know," I'd said, hating myself for it.

"What do you mean?" I could picture her quick frown, the puzzled headshake.

"Naomi heard a rumour…"

"And you didn't tell me?"

"There's always rumours, Ruby. I wanted to know whether this one was as true as it sounded." Ruby read the words I wasn't saying.

"When did you talk to him?"

"Just before lunch." I'd woken him from his hangover – word of his transgression had spread whilst he was still trying to sleep it off. "He wanted to talk to you himself."

I hadn't given Stu much choice. If he hadn't told her, I would have.

Ruby said nothing. All I could hear was the rattle of the wind as she walked.

"I'm sorry, Ruby."

"I know," she said, then, "It's not your fault I had such a suckjob for a boyfriend."

"Do you want to talk about it?"

"No. I want to watch Harry Potter."

Fifteen minutes later, Ruby was on my doorstep and we loaded up *The Philosopher's Stone*. At the end of the film, she gave me a hug and told me I was forgiven. Her ex-boyfriend was not.

Stuart Garside stopped being someone Ruby cared about when she dumped him. She deleted his number from her phone, binned all his photos and tore up the tickets of the gigs they'd been to. If she could have wiped her memories clean *Eternal Sunshine*-style, she would have. So that means she won't want to know he's here – doesn't it?

RUBY

Dongle is the least reliable informant ever. As soon as I start quizzing him about Tom's mysterious fit girlfriend, he backs down.

"Which tearooms?" I ask. There are about a million within a square mile of the seafront.

Dongle mumbles something about the one at the end of the parade.

"What were you doing in a tearoom?" Parvati hijacks the interrogation.

"I go with my nan sometimes." Dongle shrugs. "I've probably got it all wrong."

"You usually have." Anna throws a scrunched-up bit of tinfoil at him. She begins to lay meat out on the barbecue trays, and when Owen starts threading marshmallows onto a kebab stick, everyone gets distracted by the thought of eating.

Not me. I'm distracted by the thought of Tom having a girlfriend that no one appears to have mentioned to Kaz.

Not even Tom.

KAZ

By the time I get back to camp, I've yet to decide what to do about Stu … until I see Owen. Owen, who is in the same year as Stu, who took the same Sociology classes. I'm sure I've seen Stu wearing one of Owen's band's revolting T-shirts. They're lime green with orange writing and only Hydro's nearest and dearest would own one, so either Stu's colour-blind, or he's actually friends with Owen.

Sensible, keep-the-peace Owen. If there's one person I can trust on this, it will be the boy-version of me.

The second I step into camp, though, I'm assaulted by introductions. Ruby introduces Anna first, whose dimples pop prettily as she waves across at me – in direct contrast to the alarmingly cool Parvati, who gives me a vague smile from behind the kind of sunglasses my sister would envy.

The new boy, who has an entire apple stuffed in his mouth like a pig at a medieval feast, is called Dongle, and although I want to ask him the origin of his name, it'll be half an hour before he can reply. Or breathe.

Ruby sits back down and waves me into the empty chair next to her. Before I'm able to ask her whether the half-empty beer bottle clamped in her fist is her first and remind her she's a lightweight (literally), Ruby leans close and stares at me as if trying to read my mind. I panic that she somehow knows about Stu.

"How was Tom?"

I'm almost relieved when that's the name I hear.

"Um … fine?" I glance away in case she can tell that I'm all aflutter about the way he flirted with me. (Because that's definitely what he was doing. I've decided.)

"No news?"

"I don't really think so." I frown at her, confused. "Should there be?"

"So he didn't say anything about a girlfriend?" Ruby's now leaning so far over that she's about to fall out of the chair.

"No, Ruby, Tom didn't say anything about a girlfriend," I say quietly, hurt that she's pushing this particular button. It's one I've been avoiding ever since we broke up, the thought of *my* Tom being with someone else… I know we're supposed to be over and I know I'm not supposed to love him, but that doesn't mean I'm ready to pass him on to someone else. Not yet. Not whilst there's a chance I could hold on to him.

"What about Naj? Or Roly?"

I know what she's driving at, but I'm not prepared to go with her. "I don't know whether they've got girlfriends either. Perhaps you should ask them?"

Ruby looks very disappointed in me for making that joke. "Or perhaps *you* should ask *Tom*?"

I say nothing. I'm not going to. There's no need. I'd know if Tom had a girlfriend – Dad would know. Or Naomi, who knows everything, would know. Besides, even if they didn't tell me, Tom would have.

Wouldn't he?

KAZ

It does not take long for someone to suggest a singalong. This is a music festival, we have a campfire – a badly tuned acoustic guitar is mandatory. No one is surprised when the person to volunteer one is Owen.

"But it's up in the van. I'm volunteering the instrument, *not* to go and get it." He pulls out his keys and holds them up. "Any takers?"

Ruby's the one who leans over. "I'll go. Kaz, you coming with?"

The look she gives me is one of concern. Ruby wants to make sure I'm all right. Her inquisition about Tom has dampened my mood and it's this that she wants to check on, but this is the best opportunity I'll have to talk to Owen about Stu and I can't let it go to waste.

"I'm pleading intense laziness." I loll further into my chair. "Don't make me move."

Ruby shakes her head at me, tells me I'm lame. But that's it. I get away with it. As soon as she's clomped off up the hill, I nudge Owen with my toe.

"Can I talk to you for a second?"

RUBY

It's nice ambling through the field. Everyone's kind of settled in now, the camps all jumbled up and on top of one another. I pass a group of lads running down the hill with huge letters spelling out the word MOOBS in fluorescent body paint across their chests.

"Moobs for the win!" I call out as they pass. "M" stops and turns to jiggle, making me laugh. It's cool here. I feel like these are my people – even if my people vary wildly in age. The couple over there must be my parents' age, although the woman's wearing a Gold'ntone T-shirt, which makes her tons cooler than my mum.

Not that this would be hard.

Relations between us have kind of broken down after I rang home with my results. There was a moment of silence in which my mum was hoping she'd misheard before she said them out loud and my dad took the phone from her.

"They're not good enough, Ruby."

"For what?" Even though I knew exactly what he meant.

"For staying on at St Felicity's."

"I could change—"

"Now's not the time to discuss this."

Seems like we're never going to. My parents are determined to book an appointment with the head next week. No mention was made of the alternative – a Kalinski kid in state education? Unheard of. If my parents have anything to do with it, I'll be back to square one, back in my uniform and back in the classroom. And Kaz'll be in the year above. Without me.

KAZ

Owen knew that Stu was coming. He'd seen him at the Hydro gig Owen played two nights ago and they'd chatted about what they were doing for bank-holiday weekend: going to Remix.

"Did you say about Ruby?" I ask.

Owen looks miserable. "The matter of Ruby Kalinski provides a conflict of interest between me and Garside. I tend not to mention her unless I have to, so I didn't. And once I'd decided not to say anything to one, it seemed best to stay quiet to the other."

"How quiet?"

"Lee doesn't know." Owen nods across the campfire to where Lee is currently trying to throw marshmallows into the (generous) target of Dongle's gaping mouth. "Lee has been blessed with many qualities, but discretion isn't one of them."

The same could be said of his sister. Sometimes a little white lie saves a lot of hassle. "So do we *stay* quiet?"

The movement Owen makes is neither a nod nor a shrug. "Maybe it's better not to spread the drama. The others aren't exactly matey with Stu's lot and it's not as if I'll let them invite him over when Ruby's here."

I'm about to point out that he won't always be here, but

my phone goes. It's Tom, and all the other thoughts fall out of my head. I stare at his name on the screen before I remember that the done thing is to answer it.

"Hello?"

"Hey, Kaz." His voice reminds me of all the times I lay in bed balancing my phone on my ear as we talked until we were half-asleep. "What are you up to?"

Don't make yourself too available, Karizma, I can practically hear Naomi hissing.

"Hanging out at camp with everyone. Owen's friends. I think you know them. Dongle—"

"Dongle Dave's here?" Tom interrupts. "That guy's a legend!"

Unless legends are made from eating pointlessly large quantities of foodstuffs, I'm not sure how Dongle qualifies, but then Tom is proud of the fact that he can burp the alphabet. It's probably a rugby thing.

"Well, er, yes…" I've lost my nonchalance now.

"Do you mind if I come over for a bit?" Tom says. "The lads seem to be pairing off with the girls next to our camp and me and Stella—" I hear a faint *"Your name is Stella, isn't it? I haven't just been making that up?"* and a laugh that I assume means it is. "Me and Stella are feeling a bit gooseberry-ish."

I try and think back to which one was Stella, but I can't. Either way, it's not going to change my answer.

"Of course. I'll come and meet you by the crossroads." I tell the others where I'm going, and the mention of Rugby Tom sends Dongle into a chorus of delighted whoops.

I deliberately avoid looking at Lee. I'm glad his sister's not here. Better phone her, though; ambushing her with Tom isn't likely to put Ruby in the most amenable of moods.

The call goes through to voicemail. The mention of *"Stuart Cheating Shitbag Garside"* reminds me of the unanswered question of Tom's new girlfriend. Even as I'm texting her, I dismiss Ruby's doubts. So what if Tom isn't keen on being paired off with this Stella girl? It doesn't mean it's because he's already taken. It could be that he doesn't fancy her – or she doesn't fancy him.

It could be that he fancies someone else…

Like me.

RUBY

When I get back, bouncing along with Owen's beaten-up guitar on my shoulder Dick Whittington-style, I'm surprised to find Kaz missing. Before I even sit down, Lee tells me where she's gone. I try not to look too disappointed. Kaz was too lazy to come for a walk up the hill with me, but she's fine to toddle off across the other side of the campsite to fetch her ex-boyfriend? How's that for priorities?

I reach into my pocket to pull out my phone, but it's not there. Before I can panic, Dongle hands it over. "Kaz tried to call you and this thing started singing 'Sweet Caroline' at me, you loser."

"It's Kaz's favourite song," I lie, reading her message. *Sorry about this – Tom's friends have abandoned him.*

Hope you don't mind him singing along with everyone else? She's stuck a hopeful-looking emoji on the end. I wish I could punch its tiny little face.

KAZ

Stella is very attractive. She has shoulder-length hair that she's dyed a pretty pale pink and her eyelashes are impossibly long. As are her limbs. She's as tall as me and half the width, but for all that, as we're walking up the South Slope path, it's my eye that Tom keeps catching. I watch as he talks to Stella, thinking of how perfectly we fit together when his arm's around me and my fingers flex open, remembering how it was to rest the flat of my hand on his chest and feel the beating of his heart.

Tom turns to ask which way he's meant to go, his eyes lingering on mine.

The college lot know Tom well enough for me not to bother with introductions, and within minutes I lose him to Dongle, who says he's been deprived of sports talk since he got here. Stella takes a seat next to Lee while Ruby gestures at the guitar.

"Is that a guitar on your lap or are you just pleased to see me?" Dongle shouts out and Ruby flicks the cap of her beer bottle at him, catching him perfectly on the chin.

"Idiot," she says. "I was wondering whether Kaz might use it to play something suitably awesome."

If she's annoyed with me about Tom, there's no sign of it. She grins up at me as she hands over the guitar, although when I start up with the first chords of the duet from *Frozen*, she throws an empty plastic bottle at me (which is preferable to a beer cap, judging by the cut on Dongle's chin).

Ruby hates that song.

When the laughter dies down, Anna suggests that I play something we'll hear this weekend: I know exactly what to play.

RUBY

I recognize the intro within a nanosecond. "Everything Ends Midnight." My – *our* – favourite Gold'ntone song. It's not that it doesn't get to me when Adam Wexler sings it, but there's something special hearing it Kaz-style. On the track it's fairly upbeat, despite the gut-grabbing lyrics, but when Kaz takes it and turns it about, the song becomes haunting and hurty.

Watching her like this, singing, losing herself, even though we're watching, makes me feel fiercely proud. Her voice is perfect and sweet, not like anything I listen to usually, and her expression as she sings makes me feel the meaning more. Lee's heard her before, but the people who haven't are all stunned, hypnotized. Not that Kaz has noticed. She likes to sing with her eyes closed – or at the very least concentrated on the floor.

Which means she can't see me look over at Tom, watching him watching her.

The look on his face differs from everyone else's.

There's no surprise there, no growing admiration. He looks proud and sad and hungry, as if Kaz is a feast he helped prepare but hasn't been invited to join.

I don't look away when he glances over at me. Instead I think of all the times I listened to Kaz cry, rather than sing, as if I can transfer the memories from my head to his. He knows he should not be here and yet there he is, sitting right in Kaz's eyeline, collar popped on his shirt, healthy-outdoorsy tan at full peak, a clean-living and clean-shaven tick list of all the things Kaz wants in a boy.

When the song draws to a close, Lee leaps up to give a standing ovation and Parvati and Dongle join him. Anna and Owen slap her on the back and tell her she's amazing. Even new-girl Stella is clapping like she means it. Only Tom and me remain undisturbed amidst all the movement – me still watching him watching her.

KAZ

After five songs, my voice starts to go. The sun's sunk below the line of trees behind me and my audience has grown. Two girls from a couple of camps over (who I can't tell apart except for the fact that one has a fringe) asked Dongle whether we had any spare firelighters. I watched as he pushed the carrier bag filled with flammable material further back under his camping chair and invited them to share our fire instead. Given that they've brought a couple of bottles of tequila that they show no qualms about sharing, no one else objects.

When I finish the song, everyone chants my name. This makes me both happy and uncomfortable, especially as some of the older people from the other camps look over. Now seems like a good time to stop and I hand the guitar to Owen, relieved to be able to adjust my position. My left foot went to sleep during the second chorus of "Time of Your Life" and I stand up to stamp some feeling back into it.

"Encore!" Lee calls out and I shake my head.

"Time for someone else's fingers to cramp," I say with a smile.

Lee pulls a face. "Does that person have to be Owen?"

There's a beat in which I don't know whether I'm supposed to laugh, because even if it's a joke, it's not a funny one.

"What are you saying, Lee?" Anna asks, although I can tell that Owen wishes she hadn't.

"That this is supposed to be a singalong. Give that one a guitar and I guarantee two songs in and Owen'll start playing his own stuff." Lee is grinning, an air of mischief about him as he points a finger at Owen. It's not a very steady finger and I wonder exactly how many of those cocktails he's drunk.

RUBY

Lee pulls this shit on me all the time, winding me up to watch me snap just for the kick of it.

But Owen's more patient than I am.

"I'm sorry, Lee, I always thought you liked my stuff."

"I *love* your stuff!" Lee redirects his finger from Owen's chest to Owen's crotch, prompting a round of chuckles from the group.

If I could reach, I'd snap that fucking finger. Lee is not playing nice.

"Nice to know you only want me for my body." Owen's smile is forced.

I know before he opens his mouth what my brother will say.

"Well, someone's got to." Lee would never have resisted a quip like that in front of an audience as big as this one.

Only no one laughs. Not even Parvati, who might be as sharp as my brother, but loves Owen more, nor the

Tequila Girls and Stella, who all draw closer together, united by their discomfort.

In the silence that follows, Owen takes the guitar from his lap and hands it to Kaz. Then he stands, stepping over the glowing fire to walk past Lee. When my brother reaches out to catch his wrist, Owen flinches away, and Lee's fingers comb the empty air.

"O…" he says quietly, then louder as Owen rounds his shoulders and carries on walking through the gap between their tent and Dongle's.

We all have the same thought at the same time – Anna, Parvati, me – we all move as if we're going to follow him, but our paths are blocked by Lee who's standing too, but not to pursue Owen.

"I need a drink," he murmurs and bends over the cool box as Anna kicks it shut.

KAZ

There's a moment of stunned silence before it explodes into noise.

"I *like* Hydro's songs…" Dongle says to Stella, who doesn't even know who Hydro are.

"… my gaydar so needs retuning…" from one of the new girls, who'd been giving Lee more than a few surreptitious glances.

"… didn't expect this kind of drama," Tom says across the gap that Owen's left between us. I glance at him, not sure what to say.

"… such a dick. What's *wrong* with you?" Anna's shouting at Lee, who's surrounded: Anna, Parvati and Ruby, each as angry as the other.

Lee ignores them, grabbing a plastic cup and pouring some of the girls' tequila into it rather than trying to move Anna's foot from where she's planted it on the cool box. "Nothing's wrong with me. Lighten up, Anna. It was a *joke*, for fuck's sake."

I've never heard Lee swear before.

"Really? You think that was funny? Pissing all over someone you're supposed to care about."

"What's that 'supposed' to mean?" Lee's face is drawn and angry as he downs his drink.

"It means that if this is the way you show you love someone, Lee, then it's a good job you're leaving. Owen's better off without you."

There's a horrified hush as Lee crushes his cup in his fist and throws it so hard at the fire that it hits the logs and bounces out on the other side. He turns and walks off – in the opposite direction to Owen. Like a greyhound from a trap, Ruby bounds after him into the dark, leaving the rest of us staring round in confusion, Anna calling someone – presumably Owen – on her phone whilst Parvati tells her to leave him be, Dongle trying to reassure the new girls that things are usually a little less stressful and offering to top up drinks.

When Tom stands up and suggests getting some chips, I'm right there with him, noting everyone's order on my phone and collecting the money. I want out of here as much as he does. It won't hurt for us to do it together.

Little food plus much beer equals bad sprinting skills and I nearly faceplant when my foot hits a pothole. By the time a particularly kind couple wearing matching sloth T-shirts have hefted me off the floor, I've lost Lee completely.

My brother is such a dickhead.

I reach into my pocket for my phone to text that insightful comment to him, but my phone's not there. Nor is it in my other pocket, which is stuffed full of Owen's keys and Kaz's condoms. I check the ground where I fell, but I can't see anything. Guess the stupid thing fell out when I was at camp. Again. Tomorrow I'm wearing better shorts. Or possibly fixing the hole in these ones since I'm pretty sure they're the only ones I brought.

Sans mobile communication, there seems little point in looking for Lee, but whilst I'm here, I may as well head down to the toilets. It's a destination that seems inconceivably distant to all the boys pissing through the fence rather than walking the *thirty seconds* it takes to reach the facilities at the bottom of the hill. Guess if I could pee standing up, I wouldn't bother either.

It's only as I'm heading out of the loos, eyeing up a particularly pretty/pierced boy who's walking along the path into the woods that I spot a familiar face.

Owen's standing with his back to a tree, head down, staring at his shoes. He glances up, scanning the path, eyes passing over me because I'm not the person he wishes was looking for him. He does a double take, and I walk over and hug him. It's a bit Harry-hugging-Hagrid, but that doesn't matter. I might be tiny, but my love is large.

"I'm sorry," I say, wishing it was Lee saying this and not me.

Owen squeezes me a little harder, and we stay like that for a few moments more before he lets go and we both sit down on the dusty ground.

"You've nothing to be sorry for, Ruby."

"Lee does."

"Yes. He does." Owen's misery is so intense I can feel it creeping over me, seeping through my skin and into my blood, flowing towards my heart.

"You know it was only a joke, right?"

"Sometimes I think our whole relationship is a joke."

"Don't say that! Lee *loves* you."

But the word "love" has been drained of meaning after what Lee said – *Well, someone's got to.* I can't bear to think that the cheap laugh he was aiming for might have cost him his relationship.

"I know he loves me, Ruby, but that's not much consolation for having the person you worship call you fat."

"But you're *perfect*!" And I launch myself at him, my throat burning with outrage and defiance and conviction. I'm squeezing Owen so hard I'm surprised he has the breath left to laugh as he hugs me back, before gently prising himself from my clutches.

"Every word you've said is what I want to hear" – his smile is the saddest thing I've ever seen – "but you're not the Kalinski I want to hear saying it."

RUBY

Owen sends me back to the camp and tells me not to worry. I tell him he's an idiot and of course I'm going to worry. I can't face the thought of those two breaking up. Owen's like a surrogate brother – a kinder, gentler one than any of the three I've already got.

Drawing in a long, deep breath, I concentrate on the smoke and the smells and the sounds of the site around me until I'm filled with something other than the thought of losing those I love. It feels like the night's half over. The sun went down ages ago, taking my hopes of a first night full of exciting new people and sexy strangers with it.

Or not. As I catch sight of our camp, it looks as if it's grown, and from the sounds of it, the new additions might just be of the boy kind.

Maybe tonight isn't a total write-off after all.

One, two, three steps closer and—

That's when I stop.

KAZ

I do not know how Stu got here.

"What's he doing here?" Tom asks me and I frown at him, slightly annoyed that he thinks I'd know – how would

I, when I'd been queuing with him for chips all the time?

Stu and his friends (Cellar regulars Travis and Goz) were sitting round our fire when we got back five minutes ago, passing a joint round as if they'd been here all night. When Dongle started to introduce them, Stu waved away any explanations. "Kaz and I know each other from way back."

The way he said it made it sound as if we'd dated or something and I felt Tom bristle. If I hadn't been so horrified at the sight of Stu, I might have been pleased about that.

"I've got to warn Ruby," I whisper, firing off a badly typed text.

Two seconds later, I'm looking at that same message flash up on the phone by Stu's foot. He doesn't notice it, but he sees me looking his way. Murmuring something to Stella, who's next to him, Stu gets up to come over and I forget about the phone.

"Don't even think of sitting down," I say. He sits down. "What are you doing here? I told you to stay away."

Stu feigns a shot to the heart, smirking the whole time. "I didn't know this was where I'd find you. Dongle called Travis, asking him if he had any weed. Travis kindly offered to drop it off … and here we are." He leans round to look at Tom. "And Tom too. Hello, Tom."

"Hello, Garside." Even when they had a reason to get along, Stu and Tom weren't exactly a good fit.

"All we need is Ruby and it'll be like old times," Stu says. Tom doesn't look happy, and his discomfort only serves to make Stu all the more amused. "How've you been, mate?"

"I've been fine. On holiday, mostly."

"Really?" Stu sips his beer. "So it wasn't you I saw down by the pier the other day?"

Tom goes very still for a moment, then, "Probably not."

"You're right. Probably not." Stu glances at me and smiles, a flash of teeth in the glow of the fire as he stands up to leave us.

RUBY

An all-over tingle of adrenalin sweeps through me along with the deep and intense desire to try and tear all his clothes off with my teeth.

It takes a second for my brain to remind my body that we hate Stu.

Hate. Him.

As he walks round the outside of the circle, I catch sight of a new tattoo on his right forearm and I wonder what it is. Without wanting to, I think of the times I lay on his bed, tracing the lines of the one that stretches across the whole of his back with my finger...

He's looking good. His T-shirt's tight to his body and his hair's shorter, cropped close to his skull. It suits him.

So not fair that my ex looks hotter and I look crapper. I gave into the cliché and cut my hair off – not, like, *bald* but short enough that I can't tie it back – and I hate it. And I've lost too much weight. A fortnight of living off popcorn and custard creams should have made me fatter, right? It didn't. I'm a half-stone down that I can't seem to make up. My boobs are flapping around inside my B-cups and the ribcage underneath is a lot more obvious than I'd like it to be. I don't need my mother constantly commenting on how healthy my friends look to know I need to get back into eating real food.

The way my throat's squidged shut at the sight of Stu is hardly likely to help matters.

What the fucking fuckbags is he doing here?

KAZ

It's Tom who notices Ruby. He nudges me, but when I look up, the light's behind her and I can't make out her expression. I want to spring up and check she's OK, but Ruby's armour is powered by other people's perceptions. The last thing I want to do is expose a chink.

There's a glance my way that's part question, part (justified) accusation, then she's walking straight through the middle of the camp to where Stu's friends are, which is a very Ruby thing to do. Tell her she can't do something and Ruby will rush right in:

* jumping off Clifton's excuse for a pier because Callum said it was a stupid thing to do
* staying out late when she'd been told to stay in
* saying *Bloody Mary* in the mirror because she read about it in a book
* starting a petition in Year 9 for our year to be included in the Flickers/Dukes mixer disco and persuading everyone across the two schools to sign it before she sent it to the local paper.

"This should be interesting," Tom murmurs next to me.

"Something like that," I whisper back, turning my head so that my lips are level with his ear. I'm distracted from all my Ruby-related worries by the freckle in the centre of his earlobe that I have a sudden and overwhelming urge to kiss.

"I'm pleased we're not like them." Tom looks at me. "That we're not angry with each other."

"I could never be angry with you." I try and keep my focus on his eyes, but I can't help glancing down at his lips. There are freckles there, too.

"We need to talk, Kaz, just me and you. There's something I—"

But Dongle's shouting and whatever Tom was about to say gets drowned out as others take up the chant. It takes a few seconds for their timings to sync and I'm able to decipher the words.

"Spin the bottle."

RUBY

Stu hasn't so much as glanced my way since I sat down between Goz and Travis, but the second Dongle starts chanting, he looks straight up at me and the look in his eyes is a gut-punch of lust to the stomach. I grab the fresh bottle of beer that Goz has just opened for himself.

My need is greater than his.

KAZ

As everyone shuffles into position, I force myself not to look at Tom, lest he see how much hope I've got pinned on this. Maybe a kiss will unlock the promise of all those shared looks, the whispers that are a little closer than necessary, the touches that don't need to be made.

Maybe this is my chance to win him back.

It's only once I look around the group that it occurs to me that the odds are not in my favour. I've as much chance of kissing Stu as I have of kissing Tom.

All of a sudden this has gone from looking like the best idea in the world to the worst.

"What happens if you don't want to kiss someone?" I hiss at Anna, who's moved next to me.

Anna rolls her eyes. "I say that every single time Dongle tries to play this game."

"Does it happen a lot?"

"Every time he's drunk and Parvati's within kissing distance." I must look as incredulous as I feel. "They went out for, like, half an hour about two years ago and he's been desperate to convince her what she's missing out on ever since. I don't know why we need to bother with the bottle charade. The pair of them'll shag before the weekend's over anyway."

"Really?"

"They usually do." Anna sighs and sips her beer and looks at me closely. "Who is it you're worried about kissing? Your ex?" She glances over my shoulder at Tom, who's helping clear up some of the rubbish from the middle of the circle.

"Someone else's," I say, nodding at Stu.

"Who'd he go out with?" Anna asks before she sees where my gaze has shifted and the colour drains from her face. "*Shit.*"

RUBY

"So here are the rules." Dongle claps his hands and everyone falls into a silence mellowed by drugs and alcohol. "You spin the bottle, you kiss the person it lands on. That person gets the next spin."

"Some of us need vetoes!" Anna shouts and I see her glance at Kaz. "No way am I prepared to snog your ugly mug, Dongle."

"And I'm not kissing any guys," Travis adds, getting a well-deserved eye roll from the rest of us. "What? I'm not gay."

"Shut up, Travis," Stu says, blowing out a stream of smoke. "Or I'll kiss that disgust right off your pretty little face."

There's a lot of laughter and a couple of good-natured threats thrown back and forth before Anna brings the conversation back round to the vetoes.

"Anyone not prepared to pucker up drinks a shot of tequila instead," Anna says.

Kaz shakes her head too violently, which only attracts unwanted attention.

KAZ

"Who is it you're so keen to avoid kissing, Kaz? It can't possibly be the boy next to you," Stu says, loud enough that everyone turns to stare at me as I'm consumed by flames of embarrassment. I can't even bear to look at Tom.

"It's you she doesn't want to kiss, asshat." These are the first words Ruby's said to him since she arrived.

"And what about you, Ruby?" Stu says in a low voice that everyone can hear.

Ruby shrugs. "Nothing I haven't done before."

Dongle and Parvati exchange a glance. There's none of the surprise that Anna displayed – they knew the score before they suggested the game. For a moment I feel like bashing their heads together.

If Owen or Lee were here, that's exactly what would happen.

RUBY

It's Stella – who's sitting pressed up a little too close to the other side of Stu – who spins the bottle first.

Goz.

Their kiss isn't anything too racy, and when it's Goz's turn, it lands on Parvati, who groans, but still goes for a snog over a shot. When she spins the bottle, it lands on Tequila Girl No. 2 and the pair of them shrug and go for it to cheers from the boys.

"Grow up." Parvati rolls her eyes at Dongle.

I lose interest in all the to-ing and fro-ing, concentrating instead on knocking back the beer in my hand and then going for a tequila rather than reaching across to the cool box behind Stu.

My attention snaps back to the game when the bottle knocks against my foot. It was Dongle's spin and the neck end is pointing at Stu. His groan is cut short as Dongle dives on him and they roll around on the floor with Dongle making kissing noises that we can all hear because his face is about a foot away from Stu's.

Stu's laughing when he's released and the sight of him squeezes at my insides.

I require more tequila.

KAZ

Ruby looks thunderous as she tips her head back to drain her cup before pouring another slug of tequila into it. I try and tot up how much she must have drunk today.

"Shit." Both Anna and Tom have gone very still on either side of me.

"What?"

Neither of them say a word and I follow their gaze to the bottle that's sitting on the rug in front of Stu. Pointing at Ruby.

RUBY

"What you waiting for?" Stu smiles across the circle at me. "Nothing we haven't done before, right?"

My words in his mouth, mocking me.

Bollocks. If I hadn't talked it up I could have just taken the shot.

No going back now.

Not that I want to. Every muscle in my body is clenched tight with excitement at the thought of kissing him. I can remember the way it feels … the way it tastes…

No way in hell will I admit to it though.

I shrug. "Whatever."

It only takes seconds for him to crawl the distance from one side of the circle to the other, his eyes on mine, but time seems to slow, the same way that the noise fades and the people around cease to matter.

My pulse starts thrumming in my throat and I swallow, the last few drinks loosening my grip on reality.

When he's right in front of me, I can't escape the look in his eyes, as if he can see my memories of everything we've done together playing on my retinas like a film reel. His clothes are infused with the warm smell of weed and wood smoke. I breathe in a short, shallow breath and taste the memory of sun on his skin and the beer on his breath.

"Come here, then," Stu says in a low voice, a murmur that no one but me can hear. That no one but me has heard before. He raises a hand to my jaw, his fingers brushing my hair back off my face and behind my ear as he brings his face to mine, his nose brushing my cheek and I don't mean for my lips to part, but…

I can't do this.

No one seems to know what happened. One minute Stu's about to kiss her, the next Ruby's leaped up and away from him, downing her drink so fast it spills across her cheek. Wiping her face with the heel of her hand, she kicks the bottle across the circle to where Stu's sitting back on his heels.

"Spin it again."

And she's gone, fast, unsteady steps on legs that look thin and cold and white in the dark night. When I look over at Stu, all he does is shrug. It's only as I'm running after her, following a rushed goodbye to Tom and a hop and skip over the guy ropes blocking my path, that I realize that Stu might have looked like he couldn't care less, but it's the first time he hasn't been smiling about something.

Good.

10 • BIGMOUTH STRIKES AGAIN

RUBY

"Ruby!"

I can't even identify the emotions that are flooding through me at the sound of my name.

"Ruby – wait!"

All I do know is that the person calling me is Kaz – not Stu – and she's not the one I'm running from. Within seconds, Kaz has caught up with me and I feel her arms round me, pulling me in for a hug that's more reassuring for her than it is for me.

"Are you OK?"

"No. I'm not OK." I glare at her, too angry with what's just happened for it not to spill out into everything I see or hear or touch. "What the fuck was Stu doing there?"

"I don't know." Kaz looks pained. "I'm sorry, Ruby." Actually, Kaz doesn't look so much pained as *guilty*. "God, this is all my fault." She almost whispers it, then, louder, she says, "I saw Stu earlier and—"

"You *what*?" I explode, my brain barely managing to process the words. "And you didn't think to mention it?"

"I did, but—"

"You thought lying was a better idea?"

"No! It's not like that. I thought maybe you wouldn't want to know."

This is the second time Kaz has decided what is and isn't good for me when it comes to the truth about Stu. At least last time she was doing the right thing. This time though… "You thought it would be better if I was totally punked by Stu turning up at my campsite instead?"

"That wasn't supposed to happen. Owen said—"

"*Owen?*"

KAZ

I hadn't meant to throw Owen under the bus (had I?), but it's too late to cover that up as well.

"I asked Owen what I should do. He said not to tell you." Oh God, I have made that sound so much worse for him than for me.

"So what? Owen is my brother's boyfriend – he's not my *best mate*. Owen can keep whatever secrets he likes from me. I didn't think you and I were meant to have any at all, but this weekend you've been stacking them up like a set of Piss Ruby Off Top Trumps. What part of 'we don't do secrets' was so fucking hard to grasp?"

"I said I'm sorry." Tears rise up behind my eyes and I blink them back down. I hate that I cry so easily. I hate that it's Ruby making me want to. "I was trying to protect you. I didn't think we'd run into him again. If I'd been there when Dongle called Travis, I'd have stopped him."

"And where were you?" The way Ruby's looking at me turns me inside out, as if my mind is a sheet of music and she's reading every note.

"I was getting chips with Tom."

"Of course you were. And when you were *getting chips* with Tom, did you by any chance ask about his girlfriend?"

"I don't need to, Ruby. Tom would tell me. It's not like with you and Stu. We're *friends*."

"Really? *Friends* – that's what you call it? Have you looked in a mirror lately, Kaz, because that dress is not a *friendly* dress. It's a—"

"It's just a dress."

"No, it isn't. Not when you wear it near him. *Come and see our camp, Tom!*" She sounds so much like Lee did and I wonder whether she has any sense of how mean all that tequila has made her. *"Let's go get chips, Tom! I love the way your trousers look, Tom!"*

I really wish everyone would shut up about his trousers.

RUBY

There's a moment when I can totally see there's a choice. Either I can a) stop shouting at the person I love the most in the world and apologize, or I can b) carrying on shouting.

I'm not someone who knows how to stop once they've started. *"Yay, please, let's play spin the bottle, Tom!"*

"Why are you being such a *bitch*?" Kaz snaps.

KAZ

I want to snatch the word from the air and crush it in my

fist until there's nothing but a corpse of letters smeared in my palm. But that's not how words work. Once you let them out, you can't take them back.

RUBY

We're in free fall.

"I'm not being a bitch!" I say, barely believing Kaz even said that word. "I'm being a *friend*!"

"Really? Because right now you're just being poisonous. What has Tom ever done to you to make you hate him like this?" Kaz is properly crying now, but I don't know if it's anger or sadness or both. And I don't know how she can even ask me that question.

"HE BROKE YOUR HEART!" I hadn't meant to shout that loud and I can see people staring at us. "That's what he did. I spent all summer gluing it back together and you're just going to hand it over to him to smash again. When are you going to get it? Tom is *over* you. It doesn't matter what dress you wear or how much you flirt with him. *You* are not what he wants."

Even as I am shouting it, I know that it's a lie. Tom looks at Kaz the way that I want to look at Stu.

KAZ

"Why are you shouting at me about this?" I'm furious at the tears that have escaped and I practically punch myself in the face as I wipe them away. "I followed you over here because I was worried about you and somehow it's ended up with you telling me why I'm the one who's a mess."

Ruby looks confused as if she's lost her train of thought and it's like I've pulled a plug – I can actually *see* the fight draining out of her.

RUBY

I try to backtrack through the words that brought us here, but when I look for them, they're jumbled and nonsensical and I realize that all the beer and tequila haven't so much caught up with me as overtaken me.

Kaz doesn't drink. Ever. And when she looks at me, it's no longer with guilt, but with disapproval. Just like that, the conversation pivots under me and I find I'm the one holding the shitty end of the stick.

"I know you're not OK, Ruby. But I don't know why." Her voice is bordering on kind, but her expression is hard, patience stretched thin. "Shout all you like about Tom – or maybe wait until you're sober and use your indoor voice. But that's not why you bolted from the campsite. What's going on with you and Stu?"

Kaz plants her hands firmly on my shoulders, holding me steady. She's so close I can't really see anything else.

"Ruby." Kaz looks at me. "Tell me."

But what am I supposed to say other than the truth?

"There's nothing going on with me and Stu. I couldn't kiss him, that's all."

I don't tell her that the reason is because I wanted to.

Ruby says nothing more, just starts walking back to camp, and since I don't seem to have any other option, I walk with her. When Ruby clams up, there's no point trying to prise her open and even if we're not walking arm in arm, at least we're not walking alone. Camp is deserted when we get there, tents zipped shut like mouths keeping secrets, and someone's stamped down on the ashes of Owen's fire. Ruby looks like the (barely) walking dead as she struggles to pull off her vest. It's not unusual for her to hit a wall after a night out and usually I'd be tutting at her, untangling her hair when it gets caught in a zip or reminding her to remove her make-up.

Not tonight.

We brush our teeth, taking turns to spit from our tent into the ashes and listening for a hiss of success. Ruby's more accurate than me, but then, as she says, Naomi and I didn't engage in spitting contests as often as Ruby and her brothers.

"Callum always won."

"Really?" Our conversation is paper-thin over the fissures of our argument.

"Don't let his pretentions towards being an intellectual fool you. Callum is a champion Spit Meister." It's a weak attempt at humour and so is the smile she gets for it.

By the time I've finished brushing my teeth and cleaning my face, Ruby's already down and out on her back, arms folded above her head, breathing with the kind of depth that comes with too much alcohol. The eyeliner she slicked on so thick this morning has held fast, but it looks wrong on her sleeping face, like graffiti on a statue.

When she's awake, Ruby is as big as her personality, but sleeping she looks as small as she really is. Her arms look snappable and I feel a prick of dismay at how thin she is at the moment. Without the smiles and the energy, the enthusiasm and the passion, Ruby looks … vulnerable.

As I unlock my phone to set an alarm for the morning, it buzzes in my hand.

Tom.

11 • IT'S BEEN A WHILE

RUBY

There's a rustle somewhere near by. A swoosh of the zip, a whiff of cool night air. By the time my beer-befuddled consciousness claws its way out of oblivion the tent is still. I roll over and see that Kaz's sleeping bag is open, slipper socks and pyjamas flopping out like entrails. Her shoes are gone when I pull open the front flap. Toilet trip, I guess.

Until I hear a familiar laugh.

Just outside of our camp, silhouetted against the glow of the fires beyond, I see Kaz. And Tom.

I yank the zip shut as if not-seeing can turn into not-believing.

But who am I kidding? Everything Kaz has done today has been leading to this moment with Tom.

Now it's here, I'm no longer so sure why I thought it was my place to stop it.

Tom broke her heart before, but who's to say he'll do it again? Maybe he made a mistake? Maybe he's been regretting it all summer and now he's finally got a chance to make things right?

Maybe I'm not thinking about Tom when I say that.

Go home, brain, you're drunk.

Tomorrow, when I'm sober, when I know how to use my indoor voice, I will tell Kaz I'm sorry and I will mean it.

KAZ

Tom hands me back Ruby's phone. The battery is at thirty-seven per cent and I make a mental note to remind her to take it to the charging tent tomorrow.

"Stu found it. I thought you'd rather I was the one who brought it back." He smiles and brushes a bit of floating ash off my cheek with the back of his fingers.

"I should head back." I half-turn towards my tent, but Tom lays a hand on my shoulder.

"Wait."

When I turn back there's no mistaking his expression.

"Yes?" My voice might be light, but the look I'm giving him is so heavily loaded I can barely lift my lashes.

There's a second in which he swallows and I expect his gaze to dart away, for him to remember that we (presumably) broke up for a reason.

Tom doesn't move an inch. "Let's go somewhere for a bit. Just you and me."

We make our way towards Three-Tree Field, pausing to cross the main track. Even though it's past midnight, late arrivals are still tramping down from the car park, rucksacks on, ground mats rolled under their arms as they carry crates of beer and carrier bags. Mostly it's the older crowd – people who have driven here from their day jobs – and the conversations I catch seem to be focused on whether there's space to pitch their tents. I don't think there's anywhere left unless they're prepared to camp up a tree. When I make this joke to Tom, he huffs a laugh at me.

The smell of roast pork and popcorn, candyfloss and hot chips engulfs us as we pass the food vans lining a track marked WEST WALK, fading into the night as the track peters out on the far side of the site. There's a choice between turning towards Tom's camp, or turning away.

It's Tom who decides, each step he takes pulling us away from the noise of the campsite and up a slope that starts off gentle before taking a savage turn up into a copse of trees. There's no one here and we let the hill get the better of us as soon as we're beyond the first of the trees. My hands are shaking. Every part of me is consumed by energy, my skin buzzing with suppressed excitement like it's opening night and I'm singing the solo.

"So what exactly are we doing here, Tom?" I look up at the sky, at the trees near by and then, finally, at Tom, who shrugs. The setting might be romantic, but the boy isn't. After all, this is Tom. The person who thought an umbrella was a suitable Valentine's gift "because we're having a wet February".

"I just know it's been good seeing you," he says. "I didn't know how much I'd missed this – *us* – until I saw you."

And there it is: the gulf between the way I feel about him and the way he feels about me. I've missed him every second of every day since we broke up.

And yet...

He misses me.

Tom reaches out for a hug and I go with it, putting my arms around him, resting my face on his shoulder and finally, *finally* letting myself breathe in the smell of him.

A moment longer and I'll pull away, break the contact.

It feels good, standing here on the balls of my feet, my nose pressed into the material of his top.

A second later he kisses me on the cheek.

I kiss his cheek in return.

He kisses me again, not on the safe skin on the apple of my cheek, but in the no-man's-land towards my lips.

I turn my face closer and kiss him in the same place, my lips soft, the touch a little lingering, and when I pull back, I don't turn my face any further, but rest it there, my nose so close to his jaw he must be able to feel my wavering breath on his skin.

Tom turns. It's only a fraction of a degree but enough for the skin of his lower lip to brush against mine. There isn't a sound between us as each of us hold our breath, waiting.

Did you ask about his girlfriend?

I don't think I need to.

RUBY

Apparently I went back to sleep, because I'm jolted awake by voices outside the tent.

It's Lee and I shuffle out of my sleeping bag, wanting to tell him what's happened, because telling Lee always makes things better, but the zip's only halfway open when I stop.

Opposite, Lee is in Owen's arms, the pair of them so closely wrapped around each other that they seem like one person, not two. Their faces are turned inwards, Lee's pressed into Owen's neck, Owen's hidden in my brother's hair. Even in the near-dark, I can see the muscles standing out on Lee's arm as he pulls Owen to him.

I do the zip back up, not wanting to intrude. It's enough to know that some of us are capable of fixing our fuck-ups.

KAZ

It doesn't feel the way I remember it –
    … it's subtly different …
– it feels better –
    … like he's been practising with someone else …
– and I don't want it to stop –
    … I should say something …
– but I pull away and look at him.

The half-light dims the contours of his face, softening what I see. His breathing is slow and heavy, and his eyes watch my lips. Neither of us says anything as he pulls me down the hill and towards where he's camped.

It's as deserted here as it was at ours and we ghost into his tent, Tom pulling me down against him, our bodies pressed together, fused by a kiss. Everything about this is urgent, as if there'll never be another chance – so different from all the months of hushed fumbling under the covers or on the sofa. When Tom leans over me, my spine curls to press as much of my body into his as possible. Our breathing has escalated from heavy to ragged as Tom lifts away from my mouth to kiss my cheek, working across to my earlobe, where the sound of his breath engulfs everything else.

There's no hesitation when his hand runs firmly up the bare skin of my thigh, under my dress and into my knickers and I'm tugging at his top, his belt, his trousers until he's naked next to me…

"Your turn," he breathes into my ear, his tongue brushing down my neck and across my collarbone to my cleavage. I unzip my dress, the material falling away until he's kissing skin that's not seen the sun.

My bra is off within seconds, his fingers twisting the clasp as if he's been doing it for years.

I've lost control of my body, let alone my brain, but Tom pulls something out of the side pocket of the rucksack my head's resting on.

It's a condom.

Nine months of talking and, in the end, when we actually do it, neither of us says a word.

RUBY

When I wake up next I'm thirsty.

"Kaz?" I croak, hoping that I won't have to look for my own water supply.

There's no reply and I turn my head to see her empty sleeping bag.

I don't have the energy to find a cup for myself and I let myself get pulled under the surface of the sleep that's lapping at my brain, wondering how long it's been since she left me.

As soon as it's over, Tom rolls away from me and all the things that have been masked by a soft-focus haze of lust and adrenalin become real and sharp and harsh. The elastic *thwap* as he pulls off the condom, the chill of the canvas my arm's resting against, the cramped tent and the smell of what's just happened, sweat and deodorant, the drinks Tom's had. I realize how naked I am, how tight and sore.

I pull my knickers back on, but I've no idea where that bra went. "Have you seen my bra?"

But Tom's still sitting up, his back to me, head down, and I don't think he heard me.

"Tom?" I rest my hand on his back and he flinches away.

That is not the response I wanted.

"Oh God, Kaz…" Tom still isn't looking at me. "What have we done?"

If I was feeling confident and clever, I would make a joke about the birds and the bees.

I don't.

When Tom turns round, he isn't looking at me the way I want him to.

He's looking at me as if he's frightened.

RUBY

I hope Kaz is OK…

KAZ

No.

I pull my dress on too fast and I get stuck, plumbing the depths of indignity as Tom tugs it down over my bra-less breasts because I was trying to cover myself up as quickly as possible.

I want to be sick.

"Kaz, please, let's just talk—"

"No." It's the only word I've said since he told me the truth.

"Let me explain."

"No."

"It's you I want to be with, not her."

"No."

"Does that mean...?"

I'm going to have to say something. "It means nothing, Tom. It means don't talk to me. It means I can't believe what you've done."

"So it does mean something?" Even when he's this far in the wrong, Tom can't help but try to be right.

I put my face as close to his as I can, close enough that he can't miss the tears I'm crying or the pain I feel when I say it again. "*No.*"

Spying my bra under his sleeping bag, I grab it and back out of the tent, not even bothering to check whether the coast is clear. I hurry away from him, from what we've done, from what I have become.

Even as I clear the circle of tents, I glance back, half

hoping that I will see the boy I love running after me, begging me to forgive him, telling me that he loves me, that there is something he can do to make this right...

That he didn't just cheat on his girlfriend with me.

There's no one there. Tom zipped his tent shut the second I left.

An ugly sob hiccups out of me and I nearly cannon into someone else on the path. For a horrifying second I recognize the pale pink hair, but Stella's too preoccupied draping herself across whoever it is she's walking with, and before either of them can see who's knocked into them, I've hurried past into the shadow of a nearby gazebo.

If there's one thing that could make this worse, it's *anyone* knowing what I've done.

SATURDAY

12 • HAMMERING IN MY HEAD

RUBY

It hurts.

There's a steady pulse in my right temple and my eyelids are gummed together with mascara and reluctance to function. My fuzzed tongue is stuck to the roof of my mouth and I feel like I've just exhaled gas that is one part rotten eggs to five parts processed alcohol.

Injustice flickers in my thoughts, but when I try and add up how much I drank, I get a bit lost. My indignation lowers its head and edges away, allowing humiliation to step up to the plate as I think of all the terrible things I said to Kaz. Groaning, I roll over and knock into a MASSIVE bottle of water with a paper cup resting on the lid. There's a message written on the cup:

DRINK ME

On the floor next to that, there's a packet of paracetamol with EAT ME written on it and then, (BUT ONLY THE RECOMMENDED DOSE!) in tiny little letters underneath. Kaz's sleeping bag has been neatly folded over, her pyjamas sitting on top like towels on a hotel pillow, but other than this there's no sign of her. I can't remember her coming in last night... Once medicated, I pull on Ed's massive hoodie that I've been using as a pillow and shuffle out of the tent and into the sun, prepared to ride out whatever looks I get from the others about how weird I acted last night.

Lee's the only person here.

"You look rough," is the first thing he says. I'd stick my tongue out at him, but that feels like effort.

"Where's everyone else?" I croak.

"Gone showering."

"*All* of them?" By which I mean *Kaz*?! It's not like her to shower with relative strangers, although she *is* a bit of a clean freak.

Lee can see I'm struggling with the thinking. "They've gone off-site to do it somewhere hot and private. And to pick up McDonald's."

This time I really am baffled. I lift my arm and wave at the nearest line of burger vans before I collapse onto the floor next to Lee.

"They probably wanted to escape the smell. You stink, Rubbuteo."

He might have a point. I close my eyes and enjoy not moving.

"Don't fall asleep." Lee prods me in the cheek and I open my eyes to see a wicked smile that promises nothing but pain. "I know something that'll sort you out."

KAZ

The shower is on its hottest setting and my skin's blotchy from the heat as I stand under the stream and cry.

It doesn't matter how many times I've tried to tell myself

that I lost my virginity to the boy I love, what I've really done is have sex with another girl's boyfriend.

I should have asked him.

It's too late now. The memories of what we did burst across my brain — all the excitement and desire now tempered with shame.

And misery. Because for all I feel appallingly, devastatingly guilty for what I've done, I feel sadder still that the boy I have always loved replaced me so quickly. He didn't even care enough to be honest with me.

"Kaz? Are you in there?" It's Anna.

"Yes, sorry. Coming!" I lift my face into the stream of scorching water and wash away the evidence of my misery before I switch the shower off and dry myself with the free gym towel. God bless Parvati for her expensive gym membership and willingness to give one of her promotional guest passes to me despite the fact that she doesn't even know my real name. My pass says CAROLINE on it.

The other two are dressed and waiting as I dart into a cubicle. My clothes stick to my still-damp skin as I pull them on, not wanting to delay the girls more than I have to. By the time I emerge, my top lip is coated in perspiration.

"You all right?" Anna asks, looking at me closely, and I catch sight of my mottled reflection.

"I'm fine!" I smile and nod as if moving will make it harder for her to see that I'm lying. "Just a bit hot in here…"

Parvati nods. "It's always baking in the changing room and I'm still steaming from the booze. Let's get out of here."

I wish I could stay.

RUBY

No doubt inspired by the summer that Ed instigated the Drench Ruby Rule – when I couldn't set foot in the back garden without someone throwing a bucket of water at me – Lee's idea is for me to stand by the water point in my bikini whilst he uses a saucepan to chuck water at me.

It has the desired effect.

The second the water hits my skin, my hangover's forgotten. What starts out as a "shower" soon turns into a full-on water fight, involving everyone within splashing distance of the taps, and by the time the attendant manning the water point comes over to break it up, I can barely breathe for laughing/screaming/shouting.

Mood lifted, skin cleansed, I walk back with Lee.

"Were you planning on telling me what happened last night, or were you just going to pretend everything's fine?" Lee's voice is quiet and he steps close enough that I can almost feel the water evaporating from his skin.

"I could ask the same of you." I glance up, but Lee's eyes are on the ground. He can poker-face it better than Gaga when he wants to.

"I'm serious, Pubes." Lee bumps my arm. "Parvati told me that there was a spin-the-bottle incident involving Stu. She told me you were angry that you had to kiss him."

That's one way of putting it, I suppose. The easy way.

"I thought it was over," I say, closing my eyes,

permitting myself a heartbeat of remembering.

"And it isn't?" Lee asks.

"It has to be," I answer.

Owen and Dongle are waiting outside with hot(ish) McDonald's. Parvati tells us we're not allowed to eat it in her mum's car, so we all end up sitting in a line on the wall around the corner from the exclusive gym. A group of toned and tanned ladies dressed in expensive leggings and branded T-shirts give us looks that range from disapproval to sympathy as they walk past, Pilates mats rolled up under their arms. We aren't exactly an attractive bunch: Dongle's sweating through the grey vest he put on; Anna and Parvati are still looking peaky despite the shower, their meal punctuated by the occasional sigh as if eating is tiring. Of the two of us who aren't hungover, I'm blotchy and miserable and Owen just looks plain miserable.

I don't know what Owen's excuse is, but every bite of my hash brown is a battle against the rising sickness I feel at the thought of Tom's hands on another girl's skin, him kissing her the way he kissed me last night...

When I look down, the hash brown I'm holding has turned into a potatoey mush between my fingers.

Back at the campsite, I stop off to collect my phone from the charging tent – I'll have to remind Ruby to do hers later. It's exactly the sort of thing she'll leave until it's too late. There's a new message from Mum.

Someone's written FLEAS!!! on the kitchen calendar. Am I supposed to know why? Do I have fleas? Do you? I can't think it's your sister.

I message back telling her that Morag's flea treatment is under the sink, signing off by reminding her to wash her hands afterwards and telling her that I love her. What I want to do is ring her and cry down the phone, confessing what I've done, but I'm not sure that will help. Mum is pretty hard-hearted when it comes to relationships – she was happier when I told her I'd broken up with Tom than when I told her I was in love with him and I envisage words of comfort that can be translated into the English language as "I told you so".

Then, because I obviously have a masochistic streak a mile wide, I reread Tom's messages that were waiting for me when I turned my phone back on first thing this morning, before I'd even unzipped my sleeping bag.

Kaz, I want you to know that the only mistake I've made was to break up with you in the first place. I want to be with you. Give me the weekend to make things right, OK?

The next message is shorter: *Please don't hate me.*

The problem is that I don't hate *him* – I hate myself …

His last message is shorter still: *I love you.*

… because I love him too. Still.

RUBY

The others get back just as I'm finishing my make-up. Ruffling my fingers through the back of the hair that I hate, I figure I'll do. As I've told Kaz a thousand times, it isn't what you've got that matters, it's how you work it.

The thought of facing Kaz jabs at my insides like someone's out there working a Ruby Kalinski voodoo doll. I can't stop thinking about how we left things last night – *jab* – after I took my rage at myself out on the person I love the most – *jab, jab, jab* – how I made my best friend cry because I couldn't – *carving knife of guilt straight to the heart.*

I have *got* to make this right.

KAZ

Ruby emerges from the tent dressed in her ubiquitous cut-offs and the string vest she bought last week from the Army & Navy Store, bright purple bra contrasting beneath. She's wearing a sweep of khaki eyeliner to match the vest, but it looks fresher, cleaner than yesterday's. When she sees me, she repositions the two kirby grips she's holding in her lips to look like fangs then gives me a vampire smile as she twists her hair away from her face.

This is the Ruby I'm used to.

"Present for you." I hold out a crumpled brown bag that she falls on like a starving seagull, ripping the paper in her haste to get to what's inside. It's not a pretty sight, but it's a welcome one – my plan for today is to make sure Ruby eats more than she drinks. I'm not making any excuses for her, but I don't think yesterday's alcohol consumption helped matters.

"How are you feeling?" I ask, sitting next to her on the grass in front of our tent.

"A bajillionty times better thanks to you." Ruby looks around, as if checking we're alone. We're not, but the others are clustered on the other side of the dead fire. "And I'm sorry. So sorry. I'm sober and using my indoor voice and" – she reaches out to lay her hands on my shoulders, tilting me towards her so I can see how earnest she is – "I get why you tried to protect me from Stu and that's what I thought *I* was doing with Tom, only I'm sorry, because it's not very protective to shout such mean stuff at you and a lot of it wasn't really that true, except about his trousers, and if you want to be with Tom—" She stops as I start to shake, my eyes squeezed shut against the tears that are welling up. "Kaz? Are you all right? What's wrong? Oh God, I'm so sorry."

I shake my head and a fragment of a teardrop flies from the corner of my eye. I don't say anything, but I don't need to. Ruby's there already, her arms around me so that no one else will know I'm crying. Sniffing, dabbing at my nose with one of the napkins that Ruby's shoved at me, I sit back up and face her.

"You were right. Tom's seeing someone else."

Ruby's face is a battlefield of emotions – despair, triumph, sympathy, sadness – before she settles on the safest, the one she's always latched on to because it's the easiest to feel.

Anger.

"What a cockwomble!" Ruby gently punches her fist into

her palm. "Want me to hurt him? I know how to make it look like an accident…"

RUBY

At least she can laugh. That's got to count for something. We hug again and when Kaz gives me a squeeze, she whispers her own apology.

"Sorry I didn't listen to you."

I squeeze her tight. "Don't worry about it. No harm done, right? Unless you *want* me to cause harm? I was serious about hurting him."

KAZ

But Ruby could never cause Tom the kind of pain that he has caused me.

13 • DAMMIT

KAZ

The others had already left camp when we emerged from our tent after sorting out supplies for the day ahead, then I end up losing Ruby in the queue for the arena. It's easy to do with someone her size, and five years of this happening on a semi-regular basis has made me philosophical – it's not as if she'll have gone anywhere other than through the gate.

Crowds of people are pressing in around me and I let myself drift through conversations that sound so much like the ones Ruby and I have been sharing all summer in anticipation of this weekend.

"… never heard of those guys…"

"… gutted I couldn't catch them last time they toured…"

"… you'll have to go to that one on your own, no way am I missing Gold'ntone…"

"… passed out when I stage-dived…"

"… watched it on YouTube…"

My phone goes as I'm channelled between gates.

Where are you where you where are you??? This place is UH-MAY-ZING. Meet you in first set of stalls you see. They have MANY trays of silver studs.

She's sent a photo, even though I'm about two minutes from seeing all these earrings in person. Ruby has a very specific fascination with stud earrings.

Some of us queue with decorum. I'll find you in five, I reply.

When I emerge from under the arch of the entrance, I see why Ruby was so excited. Off to the right, beyond the stalls Ruby's (presumably) browsing, there's an enormous yellow-and-blue striped tent, the roof pitched in peaks and curves like a fairy-tale palace. Directly ahead of me there's a cluster of fairground rides, sun reflecting off the roof of the waltzers and a fresh-white Ferris wheel suspending cable-car clouds against the sky. These rides are no different from the ones on the pier at Clifton, but the festival setting gives them added glamour, although the music coming from them – a cacophany of pop tunes and sound effects – seems at odds with the crowd of people in band T-shirts and festival hats.

I'm turning to look at the ping-pong tables over by the tent marked ALTERNATIVE when I catch sight of Tom.

Seeing his profile hurts like a burn and I recoil from the shock. An arena of eighty thousand and *he's* the first person I see in here? It feels less like coincidence and more like punishment. Still, the sight of him is a scab I can't resist picking and slowly, carefully, wary of the pain, I let myself look once more.

He's with Naj, who's hard to miss in his dayglo singlet. It's my bad luck that Naj chooses this exact moment to glance my way.

"KAZ!" Naj roars, disproportionately delighted to see me.

Tom looks as horrified as I feel. As he should.

My natural inclination is to smile, wave and walk purposefully in the opposite direction, but that seems weak somehow. Ruby would never be so feeble.

Inspired by the way she marched over to Goz and Travis last night, I plaster a grin on my face and walk over to join them, watching the colour drain from Tom's face with every step. My forcibly bright question about how they are prompts Naj into a monologue about his and Roly's "epic" night and the delights of a burger-van breakfast, but when I sneak a glance at Tom, he's turned ashen, as if he's incapable of emoting anything other than panic.

"So" – Naj puts an arm round me – "who are you most excited about seeing today, Kaz?"

This is awkward. Naj has never been this friendly before and I don't really want someone who smells of fried onions breathing this close to me, but it would be impolite to step away when he's holding out the programme for me to look at.

"Well, Gold'ntone, obviously." I point at the 9 p.m. slot on the main stage. "Maybe these guys. Ruby insists I should go and watch Grundiiz with her, but I'm not convinced. This girl's got a really great voice…"

I trail off as I realize that no one's paying any attention. Naj is looking at Tom, a mischievous slant to his smile, and Tom is looking over my shoulder. Glancing round, expecting to see Roly, I see something entirely different.

A girl. Waving. At us.

It's then that I notice the beads of sweat along Tom's hairline.

Seconds later the girl is ruffling Naj's hair. "Hey, Naj, and hey, you…"

She steps closer to Tom, her hand sliding up the bare skin of his arm under the sleeve of his T-shirt as she presses her lips to his cheek.

"Lauren." Tom smiles, but it's all wrong. Everything about this is all wrong. "This is Kaz. Kaz, this is Lauren."

I'm going to be sick.

RUBY

Kaz is taking ages and I'm worried she's lost, which is impressive given that the stalls are about ten bloody paces from the entrance. I take my phone out from the safety-pin reinforced pocket of my shorts and give her a call.

"Where are you?"

"With Tom."

"What?" I genuinely do not understand what is happening.

"Come and join us!" Kaz does not sound normal.

"Are you all right?"

"You can meet Lauren."

"Who's Laur—"

Ah.

KAZ

I should have used Ruby's phone call as a means of escape, but my feet appear to be rooted to the dirt beneath them.

Oh God. Oh God. Oh God.

"So *you're* the famous Kaz?" Lauren looks at me as if I'm some kind of celebrity.

"Well, I'm Kaz." A little bit of bile comes up along with the words, but I swallow it back. "I'm not sure about the famous part."

Lauren laughs and nudges Tom. "This one talks about you quite a bit."

"No, I don't." Tom looks alarmed. "Not like that."

Lauren glances at him, confused. "Like what?"

"I don't know." Tom is sweating profusely now. He's never been good under pressure. "Like anything."

Naj laughs – with his widow's peak and arched eyebrows he looks like the devil. All you'd need to do is draw a goatee and the transformation would be complete. I have never felt more like strangling anyone in my entire life.

Except possibly Tom.

RUBY

Huh. So Tom has a type. Who knew? This Lauren is basically Kaz Mark II. They're the same height and skin tone – she even has my best mate's charity-shop style.

But I'm not Tom and I don't give a shit what she looks like. Lauren is not the one I care about.

I take a big step into this little circle of hell and loop my arm through Kaz's. "Hello. Apparently I've come here to meet Lauren?"

"Hi…" Lauren holds up her hand in a hesitant wave. "That's me. And you are?"

"Ruby." I meet her gaze for a second. Lauren is as underwhelmed at meeting me as I am at meeting her.

"Nice to meet you." She tries a smile.

"Of course it is. I'm delightful." That was meant to be a joke, but Lauren looks less than delighted by me.

There's a pause in which everyone sort of avoids making eye contact whilst also looking for someone else to say something. It is the epitome of awkward.

"So…" I say, "let's never do this again. Goodbye." I do a weird circular wave with my free hand, like an utter twat, and drag Kaz by the arm as she manages a rather quiet, "Bye."

As we turn away, I keep a firm hold on her and head straight for the toilets. If I know anything about my best friend, it's that she's trying really hard not to vom right now.

KAZ

Ruby's always sending me links to interesting things she finds on the Internet. A large proportion of these are photos of a semi-naked Adam Wexler, tattoos she wants and cool illustrations and animations she's come across, with the occasional Harry Potter GIF thrown in for good measure, but there's one that springs to mind right now. It's a series of photos of different pairs of girls, each picture showing the same thing: one holding back the other's hair as she crouches over a toilet bowl with the caption *Friendship is...*

What I wouldn't give for this to be a toilet bowl.

"It stinks in here," Ruby adds helpfully, the hand not holding my hair clamped over her nose and mouth, muffling her words.

My response to her comment is to attempt yet another dry heave into the cesspool below.

"That's number six. New record," she says.

"I didn't know there was one," I whisper, my eyes still squeezed shut lest I catch sight of the things I can smell.

"There was. When you're a bit less retch-happy, I'll remind you when you set it."

I risk a breath that I instantly regret – although I'm relieved to discover that it doesn't prompt a Mexican wave of the digestive tract. "Think I might be done."

Ruby doesn't waste time saying anything, but simply pulls me back from the brink and out into the fresh, glorious air, towing me straight to the taps, where I splash water over my face until I feel something approaching human. When I turn back, Ruby's stolen some clean toilet paper from a passer-by.

"I could kiss you for this." Being sick always makes me a bit over-emotional.

"Please don't," comes the reply.

RUBY

There's nothing like salty carbs to calm an unstable stomach and we head straight to the nearest food van for chips.

"Remind me to eat something vaguely resembling a vegetable at some point today," Kaz says.

My response is to guide the chip she's holding into the ketchup on the side of the tray. "It's called tomato sauce for a reason and that reason is tomatoes."

Kaz shakes her head and smiles, although it's faded by the time she turns back from throwing the empty tray in the bin.

"So. Tom's girlfriend..." I start. There's no point dodging the issue, but I keep a wary eye on Kaz, in case those chips make a sudden reappearance. "What's she doing here?"

"Presumably watching some bands." Kaz's voice is as deadened as her expression and I'm momentarily breathless with anger at Tom for doing this to her. For leading her on like that when her replacement was planning on rocking up today.

"Where was she yesterday?" When it might have been good to know she existed. "Squashed in a pocket of his rucksack? Locked in the boot of his mum's Fiesta up in the car park?"

I get a vague smile for this. "Lauren said something about her cousin's wedding. Her parents dropped her off on the drive back."

Since I can't think of a suitably witty comeback to this, I opt for the low road.

"Whatever," I say, linking Kaz's arm in mine and moving towards the clothing stalls. "This new girlfriend isn't a patch on the last one." I squeeze Kaz's arm and a second later she squeezes back. "Plus she's as rough as a hedgehog's arse."

Which makes her laugh for a second, only for it to turn into self-doubt. "No, she isn't, Ruby. She's depressingly gorgeous. And sweet."

"Like the stench of a rotting corpse."

Another laugh, louder, deeper, like she actually finds me funny. "She seemed really friendly."

"About as friendly as…" *C'mon, brain.* "Crabs. The kind you catch off a dodgy man-whore, not the snippy ones." I make pinching crab-claws with my free hand at her until she bats me away.

She's shaking her head, but it's doing nothing to shift the smile that's growing there. "You're determined to hate her?"

"Best friend's honour."

And she stops walking and pulls me into the biggest hug I think she's ever given me. So big that I feel like I'm surrounded in a blanket of cosy-Kazness.

"I love you to bits, Ruby Kalinski," she murmurs.

"Back atcha, Karizma Asante-Blake." I give her an extra tight squeeze. People talk about love all the time, but they mean all that romantic crap that comes with sextras and heartbreak. The kind of love that drives you mental and changes you into a different kind of person – the kind of love Kaz felt/feels for Tom.

That isn't something I ever plan on feeling.

The love I have for my best friend? That's the kind I plan on feeling for ever.

KAZ

Ruby's solution to cheering me up is to distract me with shopping. When she buys a vest with a whimsical unicorn on, she haggles with the stallholder until she leaves with a bonus whimsical badger vest for me, and at the vintage clothes stall she joins me in looking through the racks of dresses rather than standing by the mirror trying on all the hats and annoying the vendor the way she usually would. It's hard to be miserable in the face of such relentless determination to cheer me up.

That's not to say that my conscience isn't putting up a pretty good fight. I'm torn between blaming myself for being so stubborn that I refused to accept Tom could have a new girlfriend, to feeling white-hot fury for how he's handled it.

He had *known* – when he held me, when he kissed me, when he tugged off my dress and ran his hands over my skin. And when he did say something, when it was already too late, he still didn't tell me the whole truth: that Lauren would be here.

When Ruby disappears behind a curtain to try on a playsuit covered in lightning bolts, I take out my phone and reread his messages.

Give me the weekend to make things right, OK?

Now I understand why that was how long he needed, given that he'd been planning on spending it with Lauren…

Please don't hate me.

I love you.

Tom is treading a very fine line between the two.

I force myself to think of them together, hoping it might work like aversion therapy: by facing my fears so I shall conquer them.

Beautiful Lauren, with her thumb hooked in Tom's belt loop.

The familiarity with which she greeted Naj.

A glisten on Tom's cheek where she'd kissed him.

Her apparently genuine pleasure at meeting me.

She seemed so *nice*.

"Are you going to be sick again?" Ruby's in front of me, the playsuit she was trying on inside out and back on the rack. I shake my head, although I keep my mouth shut, just in case. So much for my therapy session.

Ruby sighs and shakes her head, feeling my forehead

with the back of her hand as if checking my temperature. "Your condition is worse than I feared, Miss Asante-Blake. We're going to have to proceed to some mega-serious medication."

I don't think doctors use the word "mega".

RUBY

The nearest tent is the Mellow Tent, which is fuck-all use for what I have in mind and I tow Kaz diagonally uphill across the field until we're at the Heavy Tent, from where I can hear some suitably moshable music.

"I'm not sure, Ruby…" Kaz pulls back, but I'm having none of it.

"I am. Come on!" Not letting go of her, I dive right into the depths of the tent. This can only be the second band to play so far and I've no idea who they are, but it seems a surprising number of people do. The crowd's deeper and thicker than I'd expect at this time of day, but when they launch into their next song, I get why. Whoever these guys are, they're catchy.

And just like that the crowd opens up in a swell of movement and sucks us in. Keeping a firm hold of Kaz's hand, I pull her into the middle of the action, bouncing around like I know the song, grinning at the people around who actually do – and that's it, she's sold, dancing with me the way we used to when we went to The Cellar. Before Stu ruined it for me.

Music has always been the key to unlocking Kaz.

Back when we were two strangers sitting next to each other on the first day of seniors, it was the moment I asked what music Kaz liked that I saw a glimpse of the girl who was going to be my best friend.

It's not that I'm not passionate about what I listen to – I am. Find me a song to love and one listen will turn into an obsessive hour-long repeat until my body's a vinyl record and the groove's been etched into me. But my love of music is from the outside – I react to what I hear without really thinking. I just go with my gut.

For Kaz it's as much about her head as it is her heart. A song isn't just a sound that tugs at her heartstrings, for Kaz it's all notes and keys, melodies and harmonies, rhythms and patterns – she hears what there is and she hears how it's made. Music is a magic that flows through her body like blood. She's last to speak up in class, girl voted Least Likely to Say Boo to a Goose, but like last night, get music to do the asking and Kaz will show the world her soul.

We only catch the last two and a half songs by whoever these people are, but it's enough. By the time they're done, so are we.

My best friend has come back to me.

15 • SELLING THE DRAMA

RUBY

The others are on the hill. I can pick out Lee's laughter from fifty paces and Anna's Hawaiian shirt gives a handy visual aid. The five of them have spread rugs off to the side of the big screen that's halfway up the slope. It's between bands, and rather than show everyone a magnified shot of an empty stage, the screen's being used as some kind of unofficial information feed. Across the top is splashed a banner that says FESTBLOG and as we approach, the main screen invites us to send "info, jokes, pics and gossip using #festblog and the Festblog team will give you 140 characters of fame by posting the best on our timeline". When that image dissolves, it's replaced with a photo someone's taken of their mate's backside, with WELCOME TO THE GRAND CANYON scrawled in marker pen across his boxers and an arrow pointing up to his bum-cleft.

I've always wanted to see a fifty-foot arse.

Not.

Owen and Anna are standing up to get drinks and Kaz and I sneak into their spots.

"Don't get comfy." Anna's threat is entirely under-mined when she winks. And by that shirt she's wearing. It's hard to take someone wearing a luminous pineapple print seriously.

"Beer, please, bar keep." I hand her a tenner, ignoring the side-eye that Kaz gives me. The stuff in here's so watered down – and so pricey – that it's not like I'd be able to get drunk if I tried.

"No inebriation on my watch," Lee says, his head resting on Parvati's stomach.

"You'll be too drunk to see, love." Parvati leans forward to pat his cheek and I hide a smile as Dongle casts a less than subtle glance at Parvati's cleavage.

"Stop perving, Dongle," Parvati says, giving him the finger.

Next to me, Kaz seems mesmerized by the Festblog screen showing a series of selfies of boys with willies drawn on their forehead in fluorescent face paint. Next there's a survey of the festival toilets, complete with ratings. The ones at the bottom of the hill by the main stage come out best, which is handy to know.

It's only once Anna and Owen come back with the drinks that I realize what a time-suck that screen is. Just as I'm about to turn away though, it starts flashing red.

HOT GOSSIP!!!

Megan Mallory from Stays Then Leaves – MEAT me later?

There's a picture of a girl (presumably Megan Mallory) with a Photoshopped speech bubble coming out of it: *I've always been a vegetarian. Animals are sentient – y'know? How can you kill them for food?*

Kaz and I exchange a glance and there are a few other groups around us looking equally baffled. The screen flashes again and there's a photo of the same girl, jaw wide as she walks away from the hog-roast van, shovelling in what is quite obviously a bun exploding with pulled pork. A huge red arrow points at the pork. Above it are the words *PIGS ARE SENTIENT TOO, MEGAN!!!*

There's a ripple of laughter on the hill, but I don't get any pleasure from seeing a "vegetarian" I don't know eating a pork sandwich. It's not like she hunted the pig down and strangled it with her bare hands whilst filming it for a music video.

"Why do celebrities feel the need to lie about everything?" Kaz tuts like someone three times her age.

"Maybe she wasn't lying? I don't know when that quote was taken – do you?" I suddenly feel very protective of Megan Mallory from Stays Then Leaves.

"Last week." Lee sits up a bit, propped on his elbows. "It was in an interview I read online."

Owen rolls his eyes. He has never approved of Lee's gossip habit.

"It's so pointless," Kaz says. "If she'd never said anything about being a vegetarian then no one would care if she was caught bathing in a steak-and-ale pie, supping on a bacon milkshake, wearing a lambskin fedora."

"That's quite the image." Dongle closes his eyes and murmurs, "Mmm, meaty Megan…" and receives a thump from Parvati and Anna. He's lucky I can't reach.

Lee brings it back round to the vegetarian thing. "It's a case of make a story and make her name."

He has a point. Ten minutes ago, I'd never heard of Stays Then Leaves. Now I won't forget.

"Still." I struggle to grasp hold of my argument – I don't know why I care so much, but I wish they could see how pompous they sound. "What's it called? Schwarzkopf? That thing where you enjoy bad things happening to other people?"

"*Schadenfreude,*" Lee and Kaz say at the same time because they are equally gifted in the brain department.

"I just don't think it's cool to laugh at someone getting caught out." I can see Kaz is about to point out how the story started. "Even if they've asked for it."

Lee and Kaz exchange a smile that makes me feel stupid and I bite my lips together to stop anything more coming out. They don't get it. My brother's a gossip and my best friend thinks anyone entering the fame game is playing with fire and has no right to complain when they get burned. Nothing I say will change their minds about Megan Mallory bringing this on herself.

I *so* never want to be famous.

KAZ

I leave Ruby to her thirty-second sulk. For someone who likes to argue every point possible, she's never been very good at accepting she might be wrong. Instead I fall into Anna and Parvati's conversation about gender politics. Ever since we went to the gym, I've felt more comfortable around them and when they laugh at something I say, it feels less like I'm talking to my best friend's brother's boyfriend's friends and more like I'm talking to people who are a lot like me.

Without Ruby in the conversation, I feel as if I'm someone people can be interested in.

I guess there'll be a lot of that next year…

Banishing the thought, I reach over to give Ruby's hand a squeeze just as my phone buzzes a text.

Instead of reaching for Ruby, I reach for my phone.

RUBY

"You coming?" I nudge Kaz with the toe of my boot and she looks up from her phone as if confused.

"What?"

"It's ten to one and time to rock." I do a lame little dance in an attempt to lighten my own mood. That Festblog thing has dampened my enthusiasm a bit. I don't like the idea of people roving around, taking unkind pictures of unsuspecting/unconsenting folk and posting them up there for all to see.

Kaz still seems confused by whatever's on her phone. She stands up and brushes bits of dried grass from the skirt of her dress. It's not as eye-catchingly stunning as the one she had on yesterday, but that doesn't mean she doesn't look good, and when a surprise breeze wafts the material above her knees, one of the boys on the rug near by checks out her legs.

Kaz is oblivious. I'm always highlighting guys scoping her out, but she never believes me. The same boy glances up again as we walk past to where Owen's waiting for us a little further up the hill.

"He was cute," I say.

"Who was what?"

"That boy back there." I nod. "The one who ogled you." I love that word. "Ogle". It's ridiculous.

"No one ogles me, Ruby. He was probably looking at you."

I give up and change the subject. "You know me and Owen are off to see Grundiiz, right?" Because, if I'm honest, I didn't expect Kaz to come with us. She once described Grundiiz as "tedious double-bass pedalling with vocals less tuneful than Morag hoiking out a furball".

"Hm? Oh. I'm not doing that."

Thought not.

"Well, what are you doing, then?"

"Calling my mum." Kaz waves her phone. "To catch up on the gossip from her date last night. Shall I meet you and Owen by the stalls in about half an hour?"

I'm nodding, but Kaz is already wandering away, dialling her mum. "Tell Afua I say hello!" I call, but Kaz doesn't even look up.

KAZ

I feel bad about lying to Ruby, but I can't possibly tell her who I'm really calling.

Taking a deep breath, I dial Tom's number.

16 • THNKS FR TH MMRS

RUBY

I have more in common with Owen when it comes to music than he does with my brother, whose excuse for missing out on Grundiiz is some plinky-plonky lute-playing drivel over in the Mellow Tent. Owen must despair sometimes. I do and I'm only Lee's sister – I don't have to sit in a car/van with him, or hang out in his room beyond my tolerance-for-crap-music threshold.

Stu had awesome taste in bands.

"You know Stu will be in there," Owen says, as if reading my mind.

It's the first time Owen's mentioned him since yesterday's shit storm.

"Kaz told me you knew he'd be here. Don't worry about it," I say, bumping Owen's arm as we walk across the grass, my boots kicking up dust.

"I'm sorry. I should have told you," Owen says quietly.

"Doesn't really bother me." I shrug.

"It bothers him."

"What do you mean?"

"I don't know, Ruby." Owen sighs and runs his fingers through his hair. "I suppose I just mean you don't get to choose who loves you any more than you get to choose who you love."

I execute an undignified snort-laugh. "Stu doesn't love me, O."

Although that's not what Stu said that day he looked at me across the kitchen and told me he loved me and I laughed in his face.

"You're not someone who falls in love," I'd said, still laughing even though Stu wasn't.

"No, Ruby, that's *you*." He'd frowned at me a moment longer. "But I don't care. I still love you."

"No you don't."

But that had been a step too far. We were still mid-fight when he left with a slammed door, shouting "Fuck you!"

Only he didn't. That night it was some other girl.

KAZ

When Tom asked me to meet him at the first-aid tent, I thought something had happened to *him*. If I'd known it was Naj, I'm not so sure I'd have turned up at all, something I guess Tom knew. The three of them (Roly's still AWOL with the girl he met last night) were in the crowd by the main stage when a crowd-surfer knocked Naj's shoulder from its socket. He has to go to hospital – something for which he needs company.

"And you want me to go with him?" I'm incredulous. "Because I'm not going to – he's *your* friend, not mine!"

I can't even believe he's asking this of me—

"That wasn't what I was going to say!" Tom has the audacity to sound annoyed before he sees my thunderous expression and alters his tone. "Look... God, this is awkward…"

He glances back into the tent, where Lauren is hovering around Naj, who's turned pale with pain. The first-aid attendant gives us an impatient frown.

"Can Lauren stay here with you?" Tom's words rush out so fast I'm not sure I interpret them correctly.

"What?"

"You're the only person she's met here and—"

"Can't she go with you?"

"She's spent a hundred quid on her ticket and she wants to see some bands, not the inside of the nearest A&E."

"Really?" My voice is loaded with disbelief. "Even if that means spending time with *me*?" I glare at Tom. "She knows who I am, doesn't she?"

"She knows you're my ex-girlfriend." There's a subtle emphasis on "ex". "She wants to get to know you."

I close my eyes. This is a monumentally bad idea.

"Please, Kaz," Tom whispers.

I should say no, but Tom has never been someone I can refuse and there's a part of me that believes a day in Lauren's company is a fitting punishment for sleeping with her boyfriend.

"OK," I find myself saying. "Lauren seems lovely. She doesn't deserve to spend that much time with Naj anyway."

"You're a star, Kaz." Tom reaches out to lay a hand on my arm, but stops before he reaches me, a buffer of air between his skin and mine as if I have somehow switched charge. Last night he couldn't keep his hands off me – now there's a force stronger than love that's keeping him away.

I believe they call it guilt.

RUBY

Halfway through the set and I'm as far into the pit as I can get. Owen went missing two songs ago, lost in a gloriously violent mess of flailing limbs. I've already been headbutted twice and caught someone's fist in the side of my head. If my parents could see me they'd have a fit – they think a crowd like this is fuelled by hate and violence. They couldn't possibly understand that it's the opposite – it's about love for the music, love for the people who *get* it the way you do – that a mosh pit and a three-minute-thirty song can be the biggest high you'll ever have.

Poor parents, they miss out on so many of the best things in life.

As the song draws to a close, there's a surge from the back of the tent and I'm swept off my feet and pressed into the back of the man in front, his sweat smeared over my face.

Gross.

I turn to the side and catch the eye of the person next to me in the crush.

It's Stu.

For a second it's like we're sucked back in time, landing in a memory of all the gigs we've been to together. His cheeks are flushed, sweat standing out on his skin and he's grinning – uncomplicated and happy. His gig grin.

As if it's taking a breath, the crowd eases up and enough space emerges between our bodies for someone to push him towards me.

Reality rushes in and I shove him, *hard*, using all of my weight to push myself as far away from him as I can and I'm burrowing, squeezing, elbowing my way through the crowd until I'm out of the tent and under the sun once more, as far from Stu as I can get. My chest is tight with something approaching panic and I'm forced to lie flat on the floor, hoping no one has vommed there yet. Closing my eyes, I concentrate on the flashes of colours in the darkness of my eyelids, counting my breaths until they're normal again. Until *I* am normal again.

KAZ

Lauren is surprisingly easy to get along with. Even disregarding the fact that she is Tom's girlfriend and I am the girl with whom he cheated, I'm awkward around new people. Yet the girl next to me has no problem talking to me as if I'm someone she knows.

I wish I'd known her before last night.

Cold shame rinses through me at the thought of what I've done, but there's nothing I can do to change it. Either I can spend the rest of the day serving my penance with bouts of useless regret, or I can let go of the things I can't change and focus on the things I can. Being a friend to Lauren today might not make up for what I did last night, but it's better than nothing.

"What do you think?" Lauren turns to me with a fake flower garland resting on her head.

"Beautiful." I mean it – Lauren is very pretty.

"I meant for you!" She places one on my head and smiles, a single dimple emerging on her left cheek. "Let's get them."

And before I can stop her, she's bought the pair, telling me to stand still as she secures mine with grips from her own hair. Then she pulls me in for a selfie that she wants to send to the Festblog feed.

"Please don't," I say, thinking of my photo-unfriendly double chin looming over my friends on the hill like the Stay Puft Marshmallow Man from *Ghostbusters*.

"Why not?" Her thumb pauses over the send button.

"I don't really like how I look in photos," I say.

"OK." She shrugs and closes the photo, but then doesn't quite look up when she adds, "But you're a lot prettier than you think you are."

The only people who ever tell me I'm pretty are my mum and my best friend, neither of whom count because they're blinded by loyalty. I don't know what blindness Lauren is afflicted with, but I can't help feeling flattered.

RUBY

I have spent all summer shutting down my memories of Stu. Last night I fought with everything I had to stop the floodgates from opening, but after that moment in the crowd it's impossible.

For the next two minutes – let's say five – I officially

give myself permission to hurt/remember/do whatever needs to be done, but after that, I will get up and walk away, leaving the pain here, a chalk outline of misery on the grass, like the scene of a crime.

His eyes.

His touch.

His smell, just there, where his neck meets his shoulder, where my lips would rest on his collarbone and my nose against the softest part of his throat.

The way my skin would turn static when he was close, ready for the spark that came when we touched.

The time we portmanteaued our names into Stuby and couldn't stop laughing at how lame it sounded.

Talking about music, lying on our sides, noses almost touching, or in his car, the windows down and the stereo up...

Him teaching me how to peel a satsuma so the skin comes off in the shape of a cock and balls.

Showing him my portfolio of line work I'd been developing, copying tattoos I found on Google Images, geometric patterns and tessellations – drawing, drawing until I found a style of my own.

Him handing me a Sharpie marker and asking me to draw him a new tattoo and the anatomical heart I drew on his chest with an arrow through it: *Stu hearts Ruby*. A week later he'd turned my design into a T-shirt for my birthday. Just the heart and the arrow, positioned over the left of my chest. No words necessary.

The evenings when all I wanted was to be held and told

that Lee leaving my house was not Lee leaving my life and it didn't matter that I'd never be the daughter my parents wanted me to be so long as I was the person *I* wanted to be.

But none of that added up to enough to keep him faithful and I force myself to relive the memory of Stu sitting astride the wall that borders the dunes, facing me but looking through me, eyes sad, voice deadened. The chill I felt because I knew what he was going to say and the ache it turned into as he found the words to tell me that he'd slept with someone else.

I play it over and over and over and over until my time is up.

Until the memory of the time after that sneaks in. The time Stu turned up at my door. I tried to slam it in his face, but Stu was too fast and too strong.

"Please. Five minutes."

I let him in as far as the lounge, where I sat on the armchair and Stu picked the closest corner of the couch.

"What do you want, Stu?" I kept my eyes trained on the patch of carpet where Ed spilled red wine at Christmas. You can only tell if you know to look for it.

"You."

I made the mistake of looking up. Stu looked rough, dark under the eyes and more than a five-o'clock shadow on his jaw. He played with his labret piercing as he watched me.

"If you really wanted me," I said, "you wouldn't have—" I stalled … rebooted. "You wouldn't have shagged someone else."

Stu looked down at his fingers then back at me. His gaze was so sharp that it hooked into me, pulling me towards him. "You knew what I was like when we got together. You *knew* I didn't do relationships until I met you. Five *months*, Ruby. I'd barely lasted five days before then. I'd never met someone I wanted to stay faithful to—"

"Why did you stop wanting to?"

"What?" He frowned before catching up. "I didn't. I was angry – *hurt* – and I was drunk and it was too easy. She was all over me..."

"Could you stop talking, please?" I said, wishing I could erase the echo of his words in my head. "I don't need to hear this."

"But you do. I want you to understand that it meant nothing to me at all. She meant nothing." He dropped off the sofa so he was kneeling on the floor in front of me, his face level with mine.

"How is that *better*? That you were happy to throw away *everything* for someone whose name you can't even remember?" I'd started crying, wishing desperately, uselessly, that I could stop. I don't cry.

"We don't have to throw it away. I'm sorry, Ruby. I fucking *love* you." He stopped. Swallowed. His fingers rested on either side of my face, our foreheads touching as he looked me in the eyes. "I. Love. You." I blinked away the tears that blurred my vision. "I have never loved anyone before you."

But I believed him even less than when he'd first said it.

"Your five minutes is up," I said.

17 • PRETEND BEST FRIEND

KAZ

There's clusters of people spread out across the grass around the Heavy Tent and it takes a while to find a space. Once we do, Lauren embarks upon making a daisy chain whilst I hold up my flower crown, framing the central peak of the tent against the sky, and take a photo to send to Mum.

All good here. How was your date last night?

It doesn't take long for her to reply: *Good. He enjoyed the cassoulet you cooked.*

I almost choke in horror as I hammer away at my phone. *YOU LET HIM COME TO YOUR HOUSE ON A FIRST DATE? THAT'S REALLY DANGEROUS!!!*

It's like she's never watched *Silent Witness* or *Luther* or *CSI.* All of which she's got entered on her dating profile as her favourite TV shows.

Who said it was a first date?

I'm confused. Who did you send me a photo of?

That was tonight's one, the one I need the red clutch for. That *is* a first date. Last night was Tony. You'd already vetted him.

Mum has a curious definition of "vet" – I've never met any of these men.

Don't invite tonight's one round to the house.

Her reply's as fast as if she's actually sitting next to me:

Sex at his, then?

"I give up." I murmur the words as I type.

"On what?" Lauren holds up a chain of four daisies and pulls a face at it.

"My mum. She invited a man from the Internet over to her house. For dinner," I add, since I don't want Lauren getting the wrong impression about my mum. (Even though it would be an accurate one.)

"Your mum dates men off the Internet?"

"Doesn't everyone's?" I feel a bit defensive, having inadvertently opened up my mum's love life for review, but Lauren just laughs.

"I hope not! Mine's married to my dad."

Sometimes I forget that other people have normal parents. Parents who don't give their daughters boxes of condoms and rape alarms as presents. Parents who think a boyfriend in the hand is better than ten at a festival. Parents who know when the cat needs flea treatment and how to reset tripped fuses.

Even with my help, the daisy chain is only two links longer when there's an especially discordant crash of guitars that fades to feedback and people start to emerge from the Heavy Tent, surrounded in a miasma of dust and gently steaming skin.

"Hottie alert." Lauren whistles through her teeth exactly the way Ruby would, before glancing nervously at me. "Don't tell Tom I said that."

As if Tom has any grounds for objection.

"My lips are sealed." I link the ends of our rather woeful

chain together and look up. "Where?"

"Twelve o'clock. Looks kind of familiar…" She's frowning.

When I look up, my heart sinks. It's Stu. He's walking in this direction, talking to someone obscured from view by a clot of burly metal-heads wearing an ill-judged amount of black leather. The vest Stu's wearing is ripped along the seam and as he twists to say something to his companion, the material flaps open to reveal the dark fingers of his tattoo curled around his side like a giant clawed hand. Watching him approach is like seeing a magnet dragged through iron filings with every girl's attention aligning as he passes.

Next to me, Lauren murmurs, "Be still, my beating ovaries." Which I find disappointing – I always imagine a Venn diagram of people who fancy Stu and people who fancy Tom to be two entirely exclusive circles.

"You know Stuart Garside, then?" I ask, surprised. Lauren told me she lives in the next town inland and goes to a completely different school from anyone I know in Clifton.

Lauren waggles her hand. "I know the name. And the face."

I guess Stu's reputation carries further than I thought.

"Who's that he's with?" she asks, and with dismay I realize who it is.

"That's Owen," I say. "One of the boys we're camping with."

Owen and Stu are about to walk right past us when Lauren asks, "Shouldn't you say something?"

Reluctantly, I stand and call for Owen.

Owen scans the surrounding area as he approaches, clearly relieved at the lack of Ruby. Stu's expression is less easy to interpret.

"Owen, this is Lauren. Lauren, this is Owen. We like Owen." Owen reaches out to shake Lauren's hand, sees the dirt that's gathered in the creases of his palm and retracts it into a wave, before wiping his hands on his shorts. Stu watches me, eyebrows cocked as I mutter, "This is Stu. We're not so keen on him."

This time it's Lauren leaning in for a handshake as she says, "Hi. I'm Lauren."

Stu meets her eye. "Oh, I know who you are." Lauren blinks at him in flattered surprise so that she doesn't see his attention flicker to me. "I know your boyfriend, Tom."

I think back to the undercurrent of unspoken things that passed between him and Tom last night and I feel like strangling him. And Tom. And possibly myself for being so stupid. I'm very throttle-happy today.

Lauren is so flummoxed by this recognition that when Stu asks where Tom is, I'm the one forced to reply – although my one-word answer of "Hospital" is enough to prompt Lauren into a lengthier explanation.

"… Kaz has been awesome, letting me tag along with her so I might actually get to see some bands. Plus it's about time we got to know each other." She beams brightly in my direction as if I'm someone worthy of knowing.

I feel anything but and when Stu's eyes flash with amusement, the thought of him seeing the way I was around Tom last night crawls under my skin until I actually have to scratch.

"Don't you have somewhere to be?" I'm anxious in case Ruby arrives. It'll be hard enough explaining the Lauren situation to her without Stu here to disrupt things. "Friends of your own to irritate?"

"You're going to have to stop disapproving of me at some point, Kaz." Stu smirks.

"Unlikely."

Owen, who has been preoccupied wiping his face on the front of his T-shirt, now clamps a hand on Stu's shoulder.

"Go away, Garside. You know who we're waiting for." Owen's warning isn't without warmth and Stu feigns injury.

"That's me told. Nice to meet you, Lauren. Later, Kaz, O…"

But as the boys clamp forearms in farewell, Owen's fingers tighten briefly around Stu's as he looks him in the eye. "I meant what I said. Steer clear."

The humour vanishes from Stu's face so that I almost see something real in his eyes – something that has more in common with hurt than with anger. "I thought we were friends?"

"We are." Owen relaxes his grip and steps away. "But family comes first."

"You and Lee get married on the sly, did you?" Stu waves away whatever reply Owen was about to make. "I get it: stay away from Ruby. First Kaz, now you – you want a go, Lauren?"

But Lauren holds her hands up in surrender. "I'm just a

bystander. I literally have no idea what any of this is about."

"Guess Kaz has some explaining to do." Stu's eyes bore into me for a moment, before he turns away, his gait more predatory than ever.

"What were you doing fraternizing with the enemy?" I say to Owen, aware that Lauren's attention is still focused on Stu's diminishing figure.

"Stu's not the enemy, Kaz." Owen looks at me carefully. "Just because someone makes a bad boyfriend, doesn't make them a bad person."

"Whatever he is, Stu's bad news," I mutter.

RUBY

I hold on to the thick wire supporting the Heavy Tent and watch as he talks to them. In a moment, I will worry about what Lauren's doing there, but for now, the only person I have eyes for is Stu.

Whatever I'm feeling, it can't be healthy, or I wouldn't feel so faint.

Alternatively, perhaps I need to eat.

My throat closes at the thought of food, my body reverting to the weird kind of lockdown it went into after I dumped Stu.

I'm not sure whether my hands are clamped so tight around the guy rope because I'd crumple to the ground without the support, or because it's an anchor stopping me from getting swept over to Stu on a wave of weak willpower.

He's leaving now, sent away before I get there, by

Owen or Kaz, not by Lauren, judging by the way her gaze follows him. It'd be hypocritical of me to criticize her for it as I watch him prowl through the crowd.

For a moment, just before he turns around the corner of the stalls towards the main stage, Stu's eyes slide in my direction.

We stare at each other for a fraction of a second.

Then he's gone, walking away with the crowd, and whatever spell he had on me vanishes with the sight of him.

Seriously. What the fuck is Lauren doing here?

RUBY

She got my name wrong.

Rachel? Fuck. Right. Off.

"It's Ruby. As in 'Ruby, Ruby, Ruby'...?" I Kaiser Chiefs it.

Blank look.

"As in 'Ruby Soho'." Best track on ...*And Out Come the Wolves*, a stone-cold classic.

Lauren screws her face up.

"As in the gemstone."

"Well, obviously." The look I get very clearly indicates that she thinks I'm a nut job before her expression opens up in astonishment. "Oh my God, are you the Ruby that Stuart Garside was just talking about?"

I glower at Kaz for an explanation, but it's Owen who steps in. "Garside is Ruby's ex, if that's what you mean."

Love Owen for putting it that way and my heart trembles at the small sympathetic smile he gives me.

"I can't believe you *dated* him!" I am really not liking her tone. I might not be a fox, but I'm not a complete moose either. Also "dated" is a revolting word.

"We went out for a bit. It's over now."

"That's not what it looks like to me," Lauren singsongs

and I want to punch her.

"Not wishing to be rude" – *so* wishing to be much ruder – "but why are you here?"

KAZ

Ruby doesn't take the news well.

RUBY

We walk back to our spot on the hill. When we get there, Dongle moves over to make space for Lauren and Kaz and it is *very* tempting to shout across and ask if Lauren is "that fit girl from the tearooms" who he was talking about yesterday, because she's the one who is going out with Rugby Tom. A fact that no one seems to be acknowledging, because IT WOULD BE TOO FUCKING WEIRD.

That's not the only thing that's weird, because Kaz and Lauren don't just have matching taste in Toms, they also have matching fake-flower crowns. Sitting together, Kaz in a sun dress and Lauren wearing a pretty cotton vest, they look like a pair of fairies made real. All they need are the wings. I look down at the limp-looking daisy chain Kaz pushed on to my wrist, my big black boots and faded Army & Navy vest.

I do not look like a fairy.

It's a shame Lee's still up his lute-loving arse in the Mellow Tent with Anna and Parvati – kind of need someone to bitch with. I try Owen instead, although I'm not over-hopeful.

"Does she ever shut up?" I whisper, as Lauren finishes telling the tedious tale of Naj and the crowd-surfer before embarking upon some other entirely boring drama that seems to have Dongle and Kaz rapt.

"She's just nervous." He clocks my best Come Off It Face. "This is hard for her, hanging out with people she barely knows, one of whom used to..." I can't help but laugh at the sound effect he uses instead of the words and Lauren glances over.

"Sorry." I wave at her to carry on with her story. "I was laughing at Owen, not you."

KAZ

Ruby does this sometimes. Ninety-nine per cent of the time she can gel with anyone – she could instafriend Voldemort. But every now and again, as if she's proving something to herself, Ruby will take against someone. In this case it's Lauren, something about which I can't help but feel bad, since Ruby's only doing it to be partisan. (I think.) She doesn't need to be though. I *like* Lauren. She's funny and chatty – someone I could imagine being friends with. If it weren't for the fact that I had sex with her boyfriend last night.

Oh God...

I can do without added guilt over Ruby's bad attitude.

When I see her get her phone out, I fire off a message:

Could you please change out of your grumpy pants and put on your happy ones? I add in a picture of a chihuahua suspended from a doorknob by a pair of Y-fronts. Animal pictures are excellent emotional currency wherever Ruby's concerned.

It doesn't take long for it to reach her. When she checks the message, she glances over at me, eyebrows raised as she mimes slitting her (my) throat.

What's with the bloodlust? Don't you like small dogs? EVERYONE likes small dogs. Or is this more your thing?

This time I attach a hideous picture of an aye-aye and watch her try not to smile as she opens it and turns to give me a bug-eyed stare. I give her my best back.

"Are you two having some kind of stare-off?" Lauren says. I turn to answer, but Ruby beats me to it, pretending to give Lauren laser eyes, using her fingers as beams, finally mustering a smile. Or something approaching a smile. A grimace that's shaped like a smile, perhaps.

At least it brings her into the conversation …

"So what subjects have you chosen for next year?" Dongle asks me.

… at exactly the wrong time.

RUBY

Someone really needs to update Dongle on the list of "Subjects Best Avoided Around Ruby". Fiddling with the daisy chain around my wrist, I can feel Kaz's nervous glances as she tells him she's signed up for French, Latin, Geography and Chemistry. When he comments on what a weird combination it is, she steers the conversation towards wanting to be an archaeologist and I have high hopes for us veering off-topic entirely and discussing Indiana Jones films, until Lauren snatches that hope Belloq-style.

"What about you, Ruby?"

It's not fair to resent her for asking, when Owen would say that she's making an effort, but I do. "Not sure I'll be taking any at all at this rate."

I've plucked all the petals from one of my daisies and I look up from the bald yellow seed head to catch a glimmer of confusion on Lauren's face before Kaz jumps in with an explanation.

"Ruby's just being melodramatic." She smiles at me to take the sting out of it. Not that it works. "Your results weren't *that* bad!"

I know she's trying to big me up, but all it does is make me feel that much smaller.

"They were bad enough that Flickers won't let me stay on for sixth form. They have standards and I don't meet them." I never have. Standards aren't something I've ever taken seriously. "The only way I get to go is if I stay back a year and resit." I concentrate on my daisy-bracelet, ripping out petals in chunks as I carry on speaking. "Either that, or I'll be heading over to Canterbury to do something less academic and more useful."

"Oh." Lauren actually sounds like she might be disappointed for me. "That's a shame."

She earns a smile for that and I shrug, saying, "It's cool. I think I'd like it there."

Now she's looking uncomfortable. "I meant it's a shame that you won't be at Flickers. I just got a scholarship – I'm starting sixth form in September. It'd be nice to have some friendly faces there." My face is far from friendly as she does this irritating little shrug-laugh. "Guess it'll just be Kaz."

My final tug on the daisy-bracelet pulls the whole thing off my wrist.

KAZ

Ruby must have left shortly after that. I didn't actually notice her go, but when I look up from laughing at something Lauren's said, Owen tells me that she's gone to the toilets.

"The good ones, down by the main stage," he adds with a smile before his attention sharpens and I turn to see Lee, Parvati and Anna attempting to skip three-abreast from the top of the hill. Owen's features are carefully positioned in a smile that's only surface-deep. He gets up to make way for them and in the confusion of introducing Lauren to the others I lose sight of him. When I find him again, he's listening to Anna and Parvati talk about the band and he's smiling for real. Then his eyes slide up to Lee and his expression shifts key from major to minor.

This morning Ruby said that Lee and Owen had made up, but sometimes I think Ruby only notices the things she wants to be true. Even if they made up, Lee and Owen aren't the happy couple that we came here with.

I can't decide whether it's better for her not to know, or worse.

I look over at Lauren. Sometimes it's both.

RUBY

I buy some chicken nuggets on my way back, but after one bite my body reminds my brain that it doesn't want to eat; would really like it if those two started getting along a little better this weekend…

I catch sight of Kaz and Lauren.

Would really like it if those two didn't.

Handing the nuggets to Lee, I slide into the space between him and Anna, joining in as they bitch about a series of dumb and dumber selfies on the Festblog feed. The screen does that flashing thing again and I'm prepped for getting my rant on.

Until I see the picture.

It's a promo shot of Gold'ntone – the one where the whole band's dressed in suits except Wexler, who is standing front and centre in nothing but a pair of jeans. I say this with a fair amount of confidence, since his thumbs are hooked into the waistband, pulling it low enough that you'd expect to see the elastic of his boxers … if he were wearing any.

RUMOUR HAS IT SEXY WEXY GOT A NEW TATT FOR HIS BIRTHDAY…

He turned twenty-three last month. Still totally within the realm of non-icky shaggableness, right?

"Why's everyone gone quiet?" Lauren says. Out of the corner of my eye, I see Kaz reach over and physically turn Lauren's head so she's facing the screen. "Oh." Lauren's eyes are wide. "I get it."

"No," Lee murmurs next to me as we watch badly doodled tattoos appear on Wexler's torso. "I think Mr Wexler is the one who would get it."

No one disagrees. Not even Dongle.

Wexler's picture is surrounded by arrows.

SHOULDER?

RIDICULOUSLY TONED BICEP?

ABS?

ROCK-HARD CHEST?

Then the question *OR IS IT SOMEWHERE SECRET…?* appears, typed across his jeans.

"I wouldn't mind finding out where Adam Wexler's secret tattoo might be," Lauren says.

"Get in line," I growl, intending for it to sound good-natured. I'm not sure it does.

The screen flashes red and the text appears: *DARE you to ask him when Gold'ntone appears at the signing tent in two hours' time!*

KAZ

"You're *shitting* me!" Ruby shrieks, perforating my eardrums and those of anyone else within a ten-metre (possibly -mile) radius.

"Please no…" Lee groans, palming his forehead in

despair, looking at his sister who is apoplectic with excitement. "This one's going to get herself arrested for molesting Adam Wexler, isn't she?"

"Quite possibly," I say around a mouthful of nugget so that it sounds more like "Quite woffably".

Ruby's feelings for Adam Wexler aren't exactly of the controllable kind. Obviously such a shameless display of excitement is the perfect excuse for Lee to humiliate her by telling everyone that she once cried because Callum had thrown away her special copy of *Rolling Stone* that contained an exclusive Gold'ntone interview. When Ruby looks to me for defence I join in, revealing the secret that she used to download the lyrics to her favourite song so she could get the words right when she sang along.

"Everyone does that!" Ruby shouts indignantly.

"Then why did you hide it?" Lee shouts louder and everyone laughs, Lauren loudest of all, and I wonder if the good mood Gold'ntone has put Ruby in will be enough to end to her issues with Lauren.

RUBY

Even the thought of seeing Adam Wexler onstage has been enough to set my nerves on edge – the idea of being close enough to touch him… Not that I will. I'm pretty certain fans launching themselves at their idols and licking their faces is frowned upon. But still.

Imagine. Adam Wexler. IRL. Not on YouTube. Not on TV. Not on a poster on my wall or a figment of my fevered imagination. Who knows what could happen?

"... you could say anything you liked, Lee. Ruby's obviously in some Adam Wexler-related daydream."

His name sounds wrong in Lauren's mouth and this is just my rock star crush's name. How is Kaz not freaked when she hears Lauren say *Tom's* name?

Whatever. *Adam Wexler*.

This is going to be epic.

RUBY

When I set my reminder on my phone for the signing, I clock how little life is left in my battery.

"Kaz?" I have to say her name twice because she's too busy finding some Gold'ntone songs for Lauren – who has apparently been living under a soundproof rock for the last two years since she claims never to have heard any – to notice me. "Do you know where the charging tents are?" But before Kaz can reach into her bag for the arena map, Lauren's telling her not to bother.

"I paid for one of these." She holds up her phone and I see there's something attached to it. "It's a portable charger thing. What phone have you got?"

A moment later she's taken the phone from my hand, declared that I'm in luck and plugged her charger into it.

"Er, thanks." Although now I'm not sure how to fit it back into my pocket.

"I'll take it." Kaz sighs and makes some room in her bag, from which I take one of the sunscreen pouches that she's brought for my benefit. It's industrial-strength kids' stuff for people who burn like bacon and it is *definitely* time I topped up. Since my vest is full of holes, I'm going to have to go for full-body application – something I'd usually sneak off to the toilet with Kaz to do, but her attention's back on Lauren. The pair of them are leaning over Lauren's fully charged phone, watching the video for "Tonight Too Soon". Much as I'd like to interrupt, I don't feel I can...

Which doesn't leave me with a lot of choice.

KAZ

Lauren leans into me a little, but I'm distracted by handing money to Parvati for some nachos. Those chicken nuggets have had a domino effect on everyone's appetite.

"... stripping off."

"What?" I look at Lauren and she nods over my shoulder.

Ruby's standing up pulling her vest over her head in one smooth, confident move, in a way I can barely manage in the girls' changing room before P.E., let alone in a field full of spectators. But Ruby has the kind of body confidence that comes from always being skinny. She runs a layer of sunscreen over her arms and chest and around her back as the boys in the group near by elbow each other and stare.

"One of those boys is offering to help her," Lauren narrates in a David Attenborough voice.

"Ruby often has that effect," I say.

"Really?" Lauren wrinkles her nose.

"Er...?" I don't know how to take that.

"Sorry. I'm not saying she's not pretty or anything."

"Good. Because she's gorgeous." The authority with which I say this is enough for Lauren to reconsider what she was about to say.

"Yeah, of course. She's got that whole manic-pixie-dream-girl thing going on." I'm not entirely sure that's a compliment and Lauren knows it, because she's biting her lip, but it seems we're at a level where she doesn't feel she needs to hold back. "It's just, do boys outside of films and books really go for that?"

"The ones who've met Ruby seem to," I tell her.

Lauren glances at me, then looks away. "I just think you're way prettier. You know?"

It's the second time she's called me pretty and I can't help but laugh, even though Lauren obviously thinks she means it and I feel so bad for laughing at such a huge compliment that I reach out and give her a hug.

RUBY

As I emerge from pulling my vest back on, Kaz is giving Lauren a massive hug. The kind usually reserved for real friends. Then Lee shouts, "Me too!" and launches himself across the grass to land on them, arms wide enough to squash both Kaz and Lauren in one embrace.

Enough now.

Without asking, I take the schedule from Kaz's bag, scanning the lists of bands, working out where I can be that isn't here, on this slope with that annoying girl.

The annoying girl in question leans over my shoulder and I'm tempted to flick my fist up and into her face. Violence probably isn't the answer.

"No. Way. I didn't realize they were playing today!"

Lauren reaches round and pulls the programme out of my hand.

"I was reading that."

But she isn't listening. Colour me un-fucking-surprised.

"What time is it?" Now she's twisting my wrist to look at the time on my watch.

Maybe violence *is* the answer?

"Kaz, you have to see these guys, they're brilliant. You'd love them." She's pointing at a band called Ivory Lace. I can tell by the name – and the fact that Lauren likes them – that I will hate them. Also, note the words she used – *you'd* love them – directed at Kaz. Not me.

"Sounds good to me." Kaz stands up. "Ruby?"

My lip curls with so much disgust I think I actually pull a muscle. "A band called Ivory Lace? They sound shit."

Kaz stares at me for a second, completely expression-less. "Because it's best to judge bands by their name rather than the music they play."

"I fancy the Heavy Tent anyway." Where I can go and legitimately hurt people without getting into trouble. Shame Lauren won't be there. "What about you, Kaz?"

KAZ

Is she serious?

"I just said I'd go with Lauren to watch Ivory Lace." I point at Lauren in case Ruby has momentarily forgotten who she is as well as what she just said.

"We don't have to…" Lauren starts to say until she sees

the expression on my face, then she mumbles something about needing the loo anyway and departs. As she passes the others, Lee half-turns to see what's going on, registers Ruby's expression and turns away, although by the tilt of his head, I'd guess he's still listening.

As soon as Lauren is out of earshot, Ruby lets rip.

"I can't believe you're choosing her over me."

"What? How exactly am I the villain here?" I try and keep my voice as quiet as possible. I'm not Ruby, I don't like fighting in front of an audience. "You were the one who turned it into a choice after we'd already decided what to do."

"So it's 'we' now, is it?"

"Yes, it's we – I'm including you in that collective pronoun. I thought you'd come too."

"As if. *Ivory Lace*." She pulls that face again.

"You don't even know the band, Ruby."

"I know that Lauren likes them," she says and I shake my head in disappointment.

"That's all this is about? You don't like Lauren." Ruby looks mutinous. *"Why?* I'm the one who's meant to have the problem and I *don't*," I say, surprising myself with the truth. "Why is it so hard for you? Why can't you make an effort for someone who likes *me*? You don't find it so hard to like everyone else on the planet." My voice rose with every word of that sentence and I try to ignore the glances I'm getting from everyone now, not just Lee.

I've got to stop letting what other people think affect what *I* do.

Ruby's eyebrows furrow together for a second and she

looks at me as if she's trying to fight back the words she wants to say.

"Do you really want to know?" she says, losing the battle.

RUBY

"Just tell me," Kaz says.

So I do.

"I don't like you around her." I reach into Kaz's bag and unplug my pathetically under-charged phone and walk away without looking back.

KAZ

I don't like you around her.

Ruby and I never fight. *Never*. I am the one person with whom she's never fallen out. As fast as she makes friends, she's faster to fight – I'm always the peacemaker, the Ruby-whisperer who can talk her back into being reasonable. There isn't a girl in our year who hasn't run up against one of her rages at some point and she and Stu spent as much time arguing as they did making up. My best friend gets angry with teachers, angry with her parents, angry with her brothers – Callum most of all. She spends a lot of her time getting pointlessly angry with inanimate objects that don't do what she thinks they should be doing.

Until this weekend, Ruby has never been angry with me.

As I follow Lauren through the loosely knit crowd that's gathering around the Mellow Tent, I think about what I've done to push Ruby so far, trying to work out how to fix things.

"Stop it." I look up sharply at the voice. Lauren sounded so much like Ruby. "I don't know what's going on with Ruby, but it's not your fault, Kaz."

"It must be."

"Why?" She's looking at me over her sunglasses, her eyes narrowed. "She's being a brat about the band and that's got nothing to do with you."

I don't know how I feel hearing someone call Ruby a brat, but it makes me want to try and excuse her, even if I don't believe the excuse I'm making. "I'm sure it's got something to do with Stu."

Lauren rolls her eyes. "As if she's the only person with an ex-boyfriend."

And we both look at each other, neither quite sure what the other's going to do…

Until I burst out laughing. A split second later, Lauren does the same.

Ruby may not like the person I am around Lauren, but Lauren does.

RUBY

The band on at the Heavy Tent are shit. What now? I can't be sitting on that stupid rug when Kaz and Lauren come back. I wander along the stalls, but it's a lot less fun without Kaz. Everything's less fun without her. When Kaz and I planned all this, it was an adventure we'd be having together, not apart. I know it's my fault for throwing one about Lauren, but that's only because I don't know why Kaz can't just see it for herself. Lauren is a) just not that great and b) SHE IS BUMPING UGLIES WITH THE BOY KAZ IS STILL IN LOVE WITH.

Although I have a very strong suspicion that Kaz might be in denial about Tom's uglies and their bumpage.

At the "tattoo" stall, I browse the designs on display, judging the people who've picked them for their lack of imagination.

"Are these all you've got?" I ask one of the girls at the table, who's refilling her henna pipe.

"Yeah…" She doesn't sound certain.

"Could I design my own?"

"Not really. We've got transfers we need to put on before we apply the henna."

"What if I drew the pattern on myself and you inked it?" But she's bored of the conversation and asks me whether I'm going to pick a design. The guy on the table next to her waves me over.

"What are you after?" he says. "I'm bored of drawing characters from Winnie-the-bloody-Pooh." Which sounds like an unpleasant medical condition.

He notices I'm staring at his arms, which are covered in real ink, and he stretches them out, rolling back his short sleeves to show his shoulders. I've not heard of the artists he mentions, but then I'm more into blackwork than colour.

"Do you think you could do me something huge and bold from here" – I point to my wrist – "to here?" – my neck.

"I think I could," he says.

20 • ONE MORE ROUND

RUBY

The straps of my vest and bra are tucked under my inked arm in case of smudging and I admire the design. The guy did an awesome job, using a black jagua ink rather than henna so it'll look almost real once it darkens. I love tattoos. My parents loathe them, which was one of the many black marks against Stu. Imagine how they'd feel if I'd paid his shady mate a visit and come home with some underage ink. They're going to kick off enough about this fake one. Although that's nothing compared to what'll happen when I come home inked for real the day I turn eighteen.

They won't be able to do anything about it though, will they? I mean apart from shout at me.

Why would you SCAR yourself like that?

You'll only regret it in ten years' time.

You'll never get a good job.

We watched a documentary about how tattoos are poisonous and the ink seeps into your arm and rots your brain until it falls out and you become a zombie. That's how the apocalypse starts.

OK, so I made that last one up, but they *are* always quoting documentaries or articles that prove how every life choice I've made is WRONG:

Subjects I took for GCSE.

What I want to do instead of A-levels.

My art.

My music.

My clothes.

My boyfriend…

Ex-boyfriend.

My feet have taken me back to the Heavy Tent whilst I wait for the ink on my arm to dry. A different band's onstage and it takes a few moments for my ears to adapt until I recognize the song from one of Stu's many playlists. I miss the music chat we used to have, him wanting to share his sounds with me, or spending hours arguing about my Second Album Theory, and the way songs would magically appear on my iPod days after I mentioned wanting to hear more of a particular band.

Kaz is a musical omnivore, but Stu was like me – we thrive on the meat of one genre.

I hadn't realized I was looking for him until I catch sight of him standing near one of the pillars. Seemingly alone, his hands are resting in the back pockets of his shorts, head tilted at an angle that tells me he's listening, judging, analysing.

Instead of doing the sensible thing and leaving immediately, I walk round to the side of the crowd and start edging in. It's a stupid thing to do, but I'm in a stupid mood. I want him to see me. I want him to distract me. I want him to… I have no idea what I want.

I force myself through one song, concentrating on the people in the crowd in front of me, reading the dates on the back of someone's Green Day tour T-shirt, realizing I wasn't even born then. The singer shouts out that this is their last song and I decide to wait it out. After this I will have a totally legit reason to turn round and ever so casually catch Stu's eye.

The song closes, the guitarist chucks a plectrum and the drummer launches his sticks. They spin towards the back of the crowd so that I finally, *finally* have an excuse to twist round and …

… see that he's gone.

This is my chance. I should leave now, get away from whatever incredibly bad idea/fantasy kept me here. If Kaz were with me, she'd see me straight, but she isn't. She's away with Lauren, and without her to remind me of why I should be avoiding Stu, I find myself looking for him.

As I turn for the exit, I see him there, arms folded, watching me.

KAZ

In hindsight, I'm glad that Ruby didn't come with us or she would be unbearably smug right about now.

Ivory Lace weren't *great*…

We're wandering the long way back to our spot on the hill, skirting the stalls that surround the Festblog "office" that's filled to bursting with people queuing up to pose with props in the photo booths. It's nearly four, but the sun's as aggressively bright as it was at midday and there's acres of pink and brown flesh on display. The air is filled with laughter and the smell of hot skin.

Lauren's in the middle of apologizing again for Ivory Lace's poor performance when her phone goes off. "Oh. It's Tom."

She looks at me and I give her what's meant to be a nod of encouragement, although she's already answering.

"Hey, you." The smile that breaks out across her face hurts my heart so much that I have to look away.

I cannot be here whilst she talks to him.

I rest a hand on Lauren's arm and point at the nearest distraction I can see – the Unsigned Stage sitting on top of the hill, the white arc of the awning reaching out above the main thoroughfare with the stage tucked in the back, like an open oyster shell with a pearl sitting in its centre. Lauren nods that she'll find me when she's finished and I make my escape.

It's immediately clear why the band playing have yet to be signed. The lead singer's voice is too quiet and the rhythm guitar's ever so slightly out of tune – which would be fine, if the person playing it wasn't also singing in several different keys. Loudly. I edge towards the front for a better view of the drummer, who seems like she's having fun at least. When the out-of-tune guitarist tells us that the next song is about someone in the audience, I look round to see if I can tell who it is by their reaction, catching the eye of the guy standing behind me. I smile shyly at the fleeting contact, then scan the rest of the faces. My eyes are drawn back to him and I realize with a jolt that he's still looking at me. Obviously my reaction to this is to turn away so fast that I hear the bones in my neck crunch. In the lull before the next (hopefully last) song, I sense someone stepping closer and hear a "Hi".

"Hi," I say. It's the same boy. Thick-framed glasses, the curls of his hair making a bid to escape the confines of the cut. He's about the same height as me, so my eyes can't help but meet his. Again.

I like a boy in glasses. It always annoyed me that Tom insisted on wearing contacts.

"Out of ten?" He nods at the stage.

"That depends. Was that last song about you?"

I hear a soft chuckle, then, "No. It wasn't."

"Maybe a four?" Which sounds a lot harsher than I'd usually go, but the singing is verging on painful. The boy laughs – a happy huff of breath, which I think means he agrees. The songs ends and we all clap, and someone in the back cheers, but I'm not sure whether that's in relief.

"Are all the unsigned bands this bad?" I can't think of anything else to say to keep him talking to me – it's refreshing to find I want him to.

"I hope not or the world will run out of new and exciting music."

There's an awkward silence, in which my phone starts ringing.

It's Lauren.

"Um. I've got to go," I say. "Nice to meet you." But I'm deliberately slow answering and the phone rings out.

"Nice to meet you too." He has a warm, easy smile and I like him more for it. "Although I'm not sure it counts as 'meeting' unless I find out your name."

"It's Kaz." I omit the usual "short for Karizma – with a z" and hold his gaze as long as I dare before I start smiling at the ground like an idiot. I am very out of practice at noticing boys. And talking to them.

"Sebastian." He nods and I nod. "I think you should come back here in" – he looks at his watch – "one hour and thirty-seven minutes."

"Here?" I repeat, because I'm confused.

"Here." And he traces a firm cross in the dusty ground with the toe of his boot. "I've heard some pretty good things about the band playing then, definitely better than a four."

"One hour and thirty-seven minutes?" My smile feels different. Flirty, possibly, and I start walking backwards before it blows up in my face and I come out with something weird, like "Nice glasses!" – the kind of compliment that sounds more like an insult.

Sebastian looks at his watch then up at me. "One hour and thirty-six."

And he matches my smile as I moonwalk my way into the sunshine, before I turn to hide the massive grin that's breaking out on my face.

I set the timer on my phone for one hour and thirty-six minutes.

RUBY

The game is on.

Neither one of us has mentioned last night, or our

moment in the Grundiiz crowd. We're both playing each other now, standing by the poster-lined panels around the edge of the arena, away from the crowds.

Stu asks me to turn round so he can look at my faux-tattoo. He studies the pattern as if it's real, touching my jaw to tilt my head so he can see where the design tapers up my jugular. I wonder if he can see my pulse speeding up.

"It's cool."

"Thank you. I think so too."

The way he looks at me is unmistakable and he leans in close, saying nothing, watching me. Waiting. I can't stop thinking of all the things we used to do that brought us this close, my brain blocking out the fact that he gets this kind of close with a lot of girls.

Or maybe I haven't blocked it out. When it feels this good to be near him, maybe I don't care.

"What do you think's going to happen now?" he says.

"I don't think anything's going to happen." I keep my voice calm.

Stu smiles and there's a rush of breath as if he's laughing. "You really think I don't know what you're playing at?"

"You think this is playing?" My lips are perfectly angled for a kiss.

"You're telling me it isn't? Standing *just* where I can see you in the crowd, one shoulder bare..." He gently brushes his little finger down from my jaw around the perimeter of the jagua. It takes everything I have in me to stop myself from trembling with excitement. "Wearing my favourite bra." The finger runs down from my shoulder to the top of my bra. The one I hairdryer-ed yesterday morning. A million years ago.

"What makes you think that's anything to do with you?" I catch his eye and go for a defiant glare. I'm not sure I pull it off – I'm not exactly wanting to defy him.

"Nothing." His hand sweeps under the hem of my vest, fingertips gliding up to rest in the small of my back, all the time watching my face, searching for a response.

"What are you doing?" I whisper and the corner of his mouth curls up in a lazy, arrogant half-smile as he closes the distance between his mouth and mine.

And I give in. I want him so much – so *very* much that I've run out of strength to deny it. I practically throw myself at him, ready to kiss him back, my hand tentatively shifting from the safety of my pocket towards the danger zone of Stu's body. All I can think about is what it will feel like to have his lips on mine and his tongue in my mouth and his hands on my body and I'm ready to give up the pretence when I feel him stop, his mouth resting on mine and I implode with wanting him.

Then he kisses me.

Days, weeks, a month and a half of carefully constructed defences are blown open and my hand is under his vest, gripping his skin and pulling him into me. His fingers press into my back, and his other hand comes down from its resting place on the boards to hold the back of my head and I can feel the rise and fall of his ribcage as he breathes hot and cold on my cheek—

Until he takes a step back. No longer in my hair or on my back, both hands are now resting on either side of my face in a way I don't like. This is the way he would hold me before he said something I didn't want to hear.

"What are you doing, Stu?" My voice, which I want to be breathy and sexy, sounds worried.

"Oh, you are so far from over me, whatever you pretend to everyone else." When he smiles it is a self-satisfied smirk and I want to punch him just as much as I want to devour him. I hate him and I want him and I wish I could not feel anything for him.

"What the *fuck*?" I shove him in the chest, but he doesn't move and I'm the one that bounces backwards. "You're the one that kissed me!"

"Ruby..." Stu frowns and gives me a patronizing smile. "We both know that's not true."

"You tricked me!"

"Can't trick someone into kissing you if they don't want to." He's grinning again and I want to slap him. "I know that look. Don't even think about it."

The one time I did slap him we had a massive fight about how it is not OK for me to lash out at people. And I know it isn't. I don't want to lash out at *people*. I just want to lash out at Stu. There's no one else who makes me angry enough.

"You're such a shithead!" I hiss.

"But such a sexy one." Stu edges closer and I push him away.

"Do you want me or not?" I snap, immediately

regretting it. How am I just putting it out there for him to decide?

Stu shrugs, still grinning.

All my fight evaporates in an instant. Is this really all I am to him? Just a joke, a point to be proved, a score to settle?

Well, I'm not prepared to be any of those things. That kiss, no matter how good, how much I wanted it, is not worth what he's charging.

Saying nothing, I step round him, careful not to so much as brush against the hairs on his arm as I pass. I hear him say my name, a *come on* that follows me like an unwelcome smell as I walk away from him.

Fuck him.

FUCK. HIM.

KAZ

It's peaceful on the hill without Ruby to disrupt things –
something that I feel a little guilty for noticing. When I sent
her a text to let her know that this was where we'd be, she
replied with a picture of a peculiar-looking mole, which is
vaguely promising. If she rejoins with some semblance of
civility towards Lauren, I know I won't say anything more
on the matter. The encounter with Sebastian and the feel of
sun on my skin have put me in a forgiving mood.

People are standing as far back as the big screen, waiting
for the act on the main stage, and Owen, Dongle and Anna
are somewhere in the crowd, leaving more room for me,
Lauren, Lee and Parvati. When Lauren goes to get a drink,
I stay, lying back on the rug, my eyes shaded against the
sun, letting the conversation wash over me, swelling in and
out of the music that's started up. Tom told Lauren that
Naj had only just got beyond triage, which means they'll be
hours yet – something I feel oddly glad about.

"Where's your pain-in-the-arse sister anyway?" Parvati
says to Lee, the pair of them stretched out across two
blankets.

"Back off, Parvati," Lee says.

"Don't feel you need to defend her on my account," I
reassure him.

"I wasn't." Lee is sitting up against the slope of the hill, his profile in sharp relief to the sky behind. I'm so used to him smiling all the time that seeing him sad is like looking at a different person. "Ruby's not having the best time of it."

For a moment I think he means this weekend and I'm about to point out that the root cause of that problem is Ruby herself – even she would deny the Stu excuse I keep trotting out. But as I open my mouth to say this, Lee turns to look at me and I shut it with a hollow pop.

Lee isn't talking about Remix – he's talking about the whole summer. When we put our pens down at the end of the final exam, everything was supposed to get better, but for Ruby things have only grown worse. First she had to hear about Stu, then deal with the fallout whilst I was away with the choir. Then her results came along and snatched away the future Ruby had mapped out in her head.

Whatever happens next – whether she wins the battle of wills against her parents and leaves Flickers for good, or comes back to resit – Ruby won't have me to support her at school, nor Lee to fight her corner at home. Ruby has never looked forward to her brother leaving, but now it seems like it couldn't have come at a worse time.

Four days from now and he'll be gone, and Ruby will have to face her future on her own.

RUBY

I'm steaming mad about what happened with Stu, but I don't know what to do about it. Tell Kaz that I went looking for trouble and got burned? For starters, I don't think I've quite been forgiven for the Lauren strop. *See you back on the hill* is not the friendliest text in the world and my picture of a star-nosed mole didn't even get a response. Plus Kaz is hardly likely to be tea and sympathy after all that shouting I did last night on the matter of *her* ex…

She might be more understanding if I told her the truth – that I have been totally lying to myself about being over Stu – but we all know that's not going to happen.

From here I can see Lee, Parvati, Kaz and Lauren on the rugs, and Dongle, Anna and Owen coming back from wherever they've been. I should be there, with them, not standing here watching. How did I get here? So far away from the people I want to be with.

I pull my phone from my pocket and delete the missed call from Stu and the text he sent that I haven't read. I might have deleted his name from my contacts list, but I still recognize his number – one of three that I know off by heart. I open up my list and dither between "L" and "K".

Then I dial.

"I need a hug." My voice wobbles as I try and keep it together. I don't cry.

KAZ

Lee gets up as Owen goes to sit down with a "I'm not avoiding you".

Owen's "That's not what it looks like" is easier to catch, although no one but me seems to notice. Not even Lee.

I try and catch Owen's eye, but he's looking away up the hill, watching his boyfriend walk away.

His expression is one I recognize.

Owen is looking at Lee the way I've been looking at Tom: as if he is the one thing in the world that he can't have.

RUBY

As Lee gets closer I can see he's caught the sun across the tops of his cheeks and his freckles are blurring together. He pulls me into his bony chest, arms warm and safe around me and I bury my face in his vest and breathe there quietly, letting it out before it turns into tears. When I fight with my parents about school, when Callum winds me up about things in the news or when Ed dropped me on my face during a piggy-back race and broke my nose – it has always been Lee who's there to put me back together. Guess I'm going to have to learn how to do this myself once he's gone.

"It's all right, Ruby," he murmurs, not asking me anything, letting me be whatever it is I want to be, even if all I want is to be sad. We stay like this until I feel I can talk again. I don't tell him about Stu, or how upset I am with Kaz. Instead, I ask about him and Owen, thinking of the hug I saw last night, wanting to hear something nice about someone else's life now everything in mine is going to shit. Lee tenses slightly, but he's smiling when he says he hasn't seen much of Owen, who's been "off on a mission to sweat in as many crowds as possible".

"Don't you want to see any of the bands?"

Lee shrugs pink shoulders and fiddles with his watch. "Not that fussed. This weekend is about more than the music."

"I came here to share it with my best mate and look how well that's turned out."

Lee looks at me for a moment, measuring how much I won't like what he's planning on saying. "Ruby. You're acting like a dick about Lauren. Really you are. She's harmless."

"So say you. How would you feel if Owen was hanging out with some guy who kept telling him how awesome he was at guitar, how buff he was and what great taste he has in music?"

I think I'm making a good point, but Lee looks nonplussed. "Boyfriends aren't for sharesies. But the same does not go for friends – even the ones you love best."

"Why not?" It's out before I can stop it. "How come I have to share everyone I love?"

"Everyone?"

"I have to share you with your wanderlust. I have to share Kaz with Lauren. I have to share Stu with every girl in the whole of the rest of the world."

"You didn't love St—"

"*That's not the point!*" I'm being unreasonable, but I can't help it. "I want to be enough for someone, all right? Enough for you to stay in the stupid fucking country, enough for Kaz not to need Lauren, enough for Stu to stay faithful!"

"I don't know what—"

"I just want to be good enough for a change for *anyone*." I'd even settle for it to be my parents. Tears are threatening to flood my eyes, but I refuse to let them.

"Let's go back to the others," Lee says quietly. "You need to talk to Kaz."

"Because talking to you made me feel so great." It's a mean thing to say and I deserve the look I get.

"Whatever you think that was, it was not you talking to me. It was you venting. I'm not Kaz. I'm not Stu." He steps closer, forcing me to look him in the eyes. "You are my little sister, and no matter how important you are to me, you can't be 'enough' for me to pass up on a chance to travel the world. I don't believe you want it to be any different, no matter how hormonal you're being."

I stare at the floor. The toe of my boot is inches away from Lee's left foot and I edge it forwards, gently kicking my foot against his. "Such a bloody know-it-all," I mutter and he swings an arm around me, pulling me back down the hill and whispering, "I'm going to miss you too, Rubik's Pube."

I will not miss all his stupid nicknames.

KAZ

Lauren has insisted that she can braid my hair to look just like the girl in one of the series of street-style pictures posted on the Festblog feed. I hadn't realized that by commenting how good that style looked I was asking to model it myself.

Mostly I prefer to wear my hair down.

There's no talking Lauren out of something.

Suppressing a wince at how tightly she's pulling on my scalp, I think how odd it is to be the one having her hair done. In junior school you were either a plaiter or a plaitee and I was *always* the former, and (since my previous school was even less diverse than Flickers) I was also subject to a lovely bit of racism when one girl told me that no one knew how to make my weird hair look good. The upside is that I'm pretty good at hairdressing and when Ruby had the notion to cut all her hair off, I was the one she asked to do it. Despite the fact that she hates having her hair short, it's not because it looks bad. Actually, when I catch sight of her walking towards us, tucked neatly in the crook of Lee's elbow, I think how good her hair's looking now it's grown out slightly.

I feel the tug and twist as Lauren plaits the remaining section of hair, using the last of the spare hair ties that we've cobbled together between Anna, Lauren and Dongle (who pretends they're Anna's spares even though I saw him tie his hair back at camp when he brushed his teeth). I turn round and all three of them give me the thumbs up.

RUBY

Whatever catharsis there was in my chat with Lee fell away at the sight of Lauren doing Kaz's hair. That's a best mate's job, surely?

You don't get to own her.

But there's a horrible little part of me that thinks I do get to own her, because Kaz is *mine*. Isn't the point of being someone's best mate the fact that you're the one who brings out the best in them? It's not a title given to you because you're the person they prefer to everyone else, the way little kids say that purple is their best or Marmite or their bike. It's about how you make them feel *their* best.

That's what Kaz does for me, anyway.

"You look aces," I say as I approach, nudging Kaz with my boot since my feet are the only part of me capable of expressing affection. It seems to work – Kaz is beaming up at me like we never even fell out.

"So does your left arm." Kaz's reflex response to a compliment is to pay it back straightaway, but she lightly runs her fingers over her head and adds, "The hair was Lauren's idea."

Of course it was. Lauren's saying something, but I'm thinking of all the times I've said how awesome Kaz would look with her hair back and how sad I am that she can't remember a single one of them.

"Good work, Lauren." And because I can't think of a meaningful way to say something nice, I follow this up with, "You should go pro."

At which she snort-laughs. "Yeah. Thanks."

Seriously. And *I'm* the one being a dick?

"Your 'tattoo'" – her use of air quotes makes me want to snap her fingers – "is, er, nice?"

The way her voice rises is not a compliment.

"Yes. It is nice. Not what I'd have inked for ever, but it's not bad."

"You'd seriously get a tattoo?"

Kaz is completely oblivious to the fact that Lauren's words were dipped in disapproval and rolled around in a bed of contempt when she explains, "Ruby's going to be a tattoo artist."

"'Artist'," Lauren says, using air quotes again. I regret not snapping her fingers the first time.

"Yes, an artist, as in body art," I say.

"OK..." She eyeballs me. "If that's what you want to call it."

Kaz is looking uncomfortable. She's been caught up in these conversations with me before, with my art teacher, with Callum, with my parents – with Tom. I guess it's not surprising that his bland new girlfriend agrees with him.

"I call it art, because that's what it *is*." My voice is unintentionally loud and Lee looks up, sees who I'm talking to and shakes his head at me. Stung, I raise my voice to explain for his – and the others' – benefit. "Apparently Lauren doesn't think tattoos can be art."

"Because they can't," she mutters.

"How can you say that? Who are you to define what someone else calls art?"

"You're trying to define what *I* mean by art, aren't you? Stretching it to include tattoos."

My brain skips a beat. This does sound like what I'm doing, but...

Lauren shrugs. "Whatever. It's hardly like it matters

what I think anyway." She looks at the time on her watch. "Doesn't the signing start soon?"

In one short conversation, Lauren has managed to hate on my tattoo, question the importance of something I really care about and dismiss me for caring enough to want to convince her. Now she's hauling Kaz up from the rug, saying a cheery farewell to Lee and the others and hooking her arm in Kaz's.

I hate her.

22 • LOVE IS A KNIFE

RUBY

When I saw the screen earlier, the thought of queuing up to meet Adam Wexler nearly melted my mind, let alone my pants. Now, trudging back from the toilets after washing the dried ink from my arm, I can't even summon up the kind of excitement I feel when I wear a new T-shirt for the first time. Kaz broke the seal when she let Lauren in and now all the colour's drained out of my mood – and as I turn greyer, Kaz grows brighter. I get close to the source of the sunshine as Lauren's telling Kaz she could totally get a kiss on the cheek from Adam Wexter.

"Adam *Wexler*," I say with more force than necessary as I join Lauren and Kaz in the queue.

"Wexter, Wexler, Dexter, whatever," Lauren sings. "He won't be able to resist this." And she frames Kaz's face with her hands Vogue-style, but instead of making some self-deprecating comment, Kaz is totally into it, sucking her cheeks in and pouting/giggling.

How come Kaz is deaf to all the nice things I say about her, but hears them loud and clear when they come out of Lauren's mouth?

"Pose, pose…" There's a frozen moment when Lauren clicks a selfie of her and Kaz. She does not ask me to get involved, because – as I appear to be the only one who's noticed – she doesn't give a shit about anything I do. They look at the screen and just as Kaz wrinkles her nose at the picture of herself, Lauren says, "Smokin', Kaz. They should name you a fire hazard."

God. Who says stuff like that?

And Kaz blushes like she believes it. The last time I told her she looked good in a photo, she declared she had an extra chin and deleted it from my phone, as she does almost all my favourite photos of her. If Kaz goes missing tomorrow, it'll be this one of her and Lauren that the police will plaster all over the papers.

"Doesn't she look good, Ruby?" Lauren shoves the stupid thing under my nose and I nod, barely looking.

"No better than usual." Which I only realize sounds catty once I've said it. I mean that Kaz usually looks that good, but that's not how it sounds. Lauren gives me a look and Kaz reaches for the phone to delete the picture out of habit, but Lauren snatches it away.

"Doesn't my mate look hot?"

My mate.

Lauren waves her phone at the girls in the queue behind us, who all agree, then she asks the same of a passing boy, who barely glances at the phone, but tells both of them to come and find him in Three-Tree Field.

"You're outvoted, Ruby."

I open my mouth to explain, but what's the point? Lauren doesn't listen – and when she's with her, neither does Kaz.

We move round a corner of the queue that snakes

around the barriers and I can see the band sitting at the table. The drummer looks bored, the guitarist is smiling at everyone, but he turns away briefly to massage his jaw. The bassist next to him says something and they both laugh and look along to the end of the table where Adam Wexler is holding a bra handed to him by a fan. It takes a second for me to realize that it was the one she was actually wearing as security gently guide her away. "That's for you to remember me by!" she shouts, before trying to lift her top – an act stopped before it starts by the female security guard, who looks like she's done this a million times before.

Every stupid daydream I had about meeting the man I worship seems even stupider now I'm actually here.

KAZ

Lauren shakes her head as the girl at the front is led away and looks at Ruby. "*You're* not going to do that, are you?" Ruby just stares at her until Lauren carries on the conversation herself. "The way Lee was talking it sounded like me and Kaz might have to restrain you."

"Just try it." It's clear Ruby's not joking. It's equally clear that she's not talking about anything to do with Adam Wexler, either.

Lauren gives a little frown before turning back to me. The queue moves forward, jiggling us all around so that by the time we've stopped, Ruby's behind us.

I'm actually quite relieved.

Awesome. Now I can't even *see* the bloody band behind those two vertically gifted freaks.

I get my phone out for something to do and discover that Lee's sent me a photo of him and Owen and Parvati grinning at the camera, looking very sweaty and very happy. *See how friends share!* To stop myself telling him to fuck off, I scroll back through my camera roll, deleting some of the crapper pictures until I catch one I didn't know I had on there. I tap back, trying to place when it was taken.

Last night. I can only assume my phone dropped out of my pocket and Stu was the one to find it. I wish he hadn't.

There's a series of them. The most recent is a selfie of Stu, with him looking broodily into the camera. He's smiling at something, which only makes sense when you scroll back one.

Him again. This time with a girl, identifiable as Stella by her pink hair, since the rest of her face is attached to Stu's in a full-on snog.

The one before is not of Stu. It's of me, running away, Kaz just coming into the frame as she chases after me.

I force myself to scroll back to the photo of him and Stella and I stare at it, until it stops meaning anything, until it's nothing but a set of pixels on a screen. But it isn't. It's a pain in my chest that won't go away.

He probably thought that was what my reaction in

the Grundiiz crowd was about until he saw me later, over there, by the boards, next to that row of Little John tour posters. At that point he must have realized there was no way I'd seen this picture, or I'd never have touched him. He'd let me humiliate myself, knowing it would only get worse when I found this photo on my phone.

I hate him.

Or something. I'm so knotted up that I'm not sure what I feel.

If we were alone, I would show Kaz and she would tell me he's not worth the megabytes the pictures take up on my phone. Maybe I would find the words to tell her something close to the truth. That he is worth something to me, even if I don't know what.

But Lauren.

So I do something stupid. I text the picture to Stu. I know I shouldn't, but the number's there in my head. I stab out the words *Thanks, fuckhead* and press send, regretting it immediately.

At the front of the queue, Lauren and Kaz have worked themselves into a frenzy of giggles and the first guy to sign their card looks as if he doubts their sanity. They move on, but I haven't anything to sign.

"Was I meant to pick up a card?" I ask.

"You were." It's the drummer, whose name I have temporarily forgotten.

"What's the point of a signed card?" I ask and he shrugs, looking bored. "Can you sign this, instead?"

I pull off my belt and hand it to him. It's a canvas

one, yellow, plain. The drummer shrugs again, looking marginally less bored, and signs the belt with his black marker pen.

I push the belt along to the bassist, who doesn't comment, and then the guitarist, who does, his rictus grin still in place.

"Not signed a belt before."

"You have now," I say, thinking that there must be something wrong with me – Adam Wexler isn't actually the only person I worship in this band. I love all of them, one way or another. I can't move on because Lauren and Kaz are still with Adam Wexler and I see Lauren shove Kaz forwards so she's leaning over the table next to him, posing for a photo. He's smiling and polite, the perfect rock star in all his glory. Moving in close, he says something to Kaz and I see her blush a shade deeper.

Curiosity flickers in me, but the flame's extinguished when my phone goes and I see Stu's reply.

Fuckhead. Shithead. Call me what you like. Doesn't change the fact that you want me...

The words are loaded with so much self-satisfaction that I feel sick and I dully step forwards, pushing my belt towards Adam Wexler for signing.

"I can't use this." I look up sharply, but he's turned away to someone behind him to ask if he could have a black pen for signing my belt instead of the gold one he's been using. When he turns back to me I feel a vague quiver of excitement.

Wexler is as sexy in the flesh as he is on the posters

taped to my wall. His eyes are Photoshop-filter blue and it's hard not to imagine what kind of gorgeous mess I'd make by running my fingers through his hair. The long-sleeved top he's wearing might hide that new tattoo of his, but it does nothing to disguise the shape of his body beneath.

I hadn't realized I was holding my breath.

"Cheer up, love. Whatever it is can't be that bad." He crooks his mouth in the half-smile I've seen accompany every Gold'ntone interview, but the impact is lost in my indignation. There's nothing more patronizing than the whole "cheer up, love" sentiment.

"Oh, really?" I wave my phone at him. "How would you feel if your ex took a photo ON YOUR PHONE of them snogging someone else?"

Wexler frowns and catches the phone to actually look at what I'm showing him.

"I suppose I'd feel like snogging someone else in retaliation." The look accompanying these words gives me all sorts of very wrong thoughts. Then he turns to take the pen from whichever assistant has found one and signs my belt before flipping it over and writing something the full length of it – something that's hard to read upside-down.

"Good luck getting your own back," he says with a wink. "You know where to find me."

As I wander off in a bit of a daze, I open my arms wide to read the message on my belt.

WHEN A KISS BECOMES A KNIFE TO THE HEART YOU KNOW YOU WERE IN LOVE

It's a lyric from one of their most famous songs. I quickly flip the belt over and thread it back through my shorts before I can dwell on what it says. Stupid rock-star musicians think they know the answer to everything. They know *nothing*.

23 · INTERLUDE

Ruby does not seem as excited by meeting Adam Wexler as I expected. The only conclusion I can draw from this is that she must have gone into shock. I think *I* have after he whispered in my ear.

It should be illegal for a man to smell that good.

"So what did he say?" Lauren asks Ruby as she threads her belt back onto her shorts. It looks good adorned with all the Gold'ntone signatures. Very cool. Very Ruby.

"Not much." Ruby looks up with a distracted smile.

She is definitely in shock.

189

"An anti-climax?" I suggest and she nods, smiling a little more as if she's grateful for me finding the answer.

"Well, not for me," Lauren says, shaking her head. "I didn't believe anyone could be that fit in real life."

Ruby grins. I think it's the first time Lauren's had that reaction – if nothing else, Wexler's improved Ruby's mood. "Yeah, he is quite hot."

"Totally falls in the 'would' category, right?" I say.

"The very definition of said category. In fact, I think he's the king of it." She's warming up even further and the grin stays for longer this time.

"What's this category?" Lauren asks.

I explain. "People you'd have sex with at the drop of a hat."

"Or their pants," says Ruby and this time it's Lauren who smiles.

I doubt Lauren would be smiling if she knew that the only person who really makes my "would" category is her boyfriend. And that I have. I try and bundle this unwelcome thought back into the locked compartment inside my head where I've been keeping it for most of the afternoon. Then I force myself to listen to what the other two are talking about.

"… how many people do you reckon Wexler's already dropped his pants for though?" Lauren is saying.

"Don't care so long as he drops them for me," Ruby replies.

"I couldn't." Lauren pulls a face. "If I'm having sex with someone, I'd like to feel it was because it means something."

This time my thoughts don't so much cast a shadow as suck the sun right out of the sky.

If I'm having sex with someone…

Having. Present tense.

If there was one thing that made last night ever so slightly less awful it was that Tom and I should always have been each other's first. This is the first time it's occurred to me that I might not have been his.

RUBY

Kaz has gone very quiet, but Lauren's still talking and I switch stations from concentrating on Kaz's radio silence to Lauren's blithering. "… suppose you'd know practice makes perfect, right?"

The look Lauren gives me is annoyingly smug. She is either thinking about a) me, which is both rude and unlikely – she couldn't care less about anything I've done unless it's connected to … b) Stu.

It's not the first time she's fished for a soundbite on the subject of Stu, but I refuse to give one. Lauren can think what she likes. I don't know whether she's heard the rumours of his studliness that reigned before I got together with him, or the gossip that swept in afterwards. The only people who know the truth of what happened in between are me and Stu.

Even Kaz only knows the edited highlights. She doesn't know that the first time I slept with him was so crap that I went to the bathroom afterwards and cried. Stu found me in there.

"What's wrong?" he asked, sliding onto the floor next to me, our backs against the bathtub. "Tell me."

"That wasn't great. For me." It'd been uncomfortable and tense and I felt like I'd been raked with sandpaper. I wasn't even sure if he'd actually finished, or just given up because I'd said "Ow" one too many times. It's not that it was my first: I'd done it a couple of times with my last boyfriend and it had been fine. Something I'd thought would get better when I found the right person. That person was supposed to be Stu, who sent my stomach into spasms when he kissed me. Who reduced my thoughts to gibberish when he ran his fingers across my skin. The thought of whom was enough for me to…

Reality hadn't measured up to expectation.

"It wasn't great for me either." My mouth twisted with misery at his words. "Look at me." His eyes were wide and serious, but his lips tugged into a small smile. "But it's just bad sex. That's all. Nothing to worry about."

"I don't want it to be bad." And I couldn't stop myself from crying. I felt like such a child. It wasn't supposed to be like this. It was supposed to be like on the Internet or in films.

"Listen. I've had some great sex. And some rubbish sex. And some so-so sex."

"All right, you tart," I muttered, not sure how I felt about him saying this.

"I am a tart." He smiled at my expression. "So I know what I'm talking about. Great sex isn't something magical. It's a skill you learn, not a talent you're born with. Why d'you think I needed so much practice?"

It was a joke, but it crushed me. "So it's me?"

Stu frowned. "Don't be an idiot. It takes two to tango."

"Why is our tango so shit, then?" My turn for a rubbish joke.

He shrugged, looking thoughtful before he leaned closer. "So I've slept with a ton of people – you know my number – and I've just told you I've had great sex with some of them ..."

Honestly, it felt like the worst pep talk ever.

" ... but there has been no one who does this to me."

And he kissed me, softly, just lip-to-lip, a little kiss. And then another. And another. I reached out and ran my hand down his arm, shoulder to wrist, only lightly, but the result was electric and I felt Stu's breath rush out before he kissed me again. Once. Twice.

"Sex just needs a bit of practice. *That?*" And I knew what he meant. "That shit you can't learn. You've either got it or you haven't."

I kissed him on the cheek and felt him sigh – a happy sigh.

"And we have that?" I said.

Stu's eyes searched mine. "Our first tango was a flop, but everything else is off-the-scoreboard-awesome."

And he kissed me again, harder, sending my nerves into overdrive as I kissed him back. By the time we stopped, it was turning dark outside and his dad and stepmum would be home soon. We were still clothed. Still sitting propped against the bath.

And we got better with practice. A lot of it.

That was the truth of what I had with Stu – the sting in the tail when he cheated. Everyone else might think they know what we had, but they don't.

Not that we have it any more.

What I have now is a photo of him kissing another girl, reminding me that my ex only knows how to be the kind of boyfriend that's for sharesies.

I'm not someone who likes to share the people I most want to be with.

24 • CAVALRY

KAZ

The timer on my phone is two minutes from going off and a live show of Sebastian's smile is preferable to the horrific symphony of thoughts surrounding Tom. I decide to risk it.

"Why don't we check out the Unsigned Stage?" Ruby and Lauren look equally nonplussed. "The band I saw earlier were surprisingly good," I lie.

I know that all I'd need to do to convince the pair of them would be to tell them I said I'd meet a cute new boy, but I couldn't cope with how they'd respond to each other's reactions. This relative harmony post-Gold'ntone wouldn't survive an aggressive compliment-off.

Besides, I just think Sebastian seemed nice. It's not a declaration of marriage.

In the end, it's the size of the crowd gathered outside that does the convincing. Neither Ruby nor Lauren object as I plough forwards, spreading apologies in my wake until I stop exactly where the X was and Ruby walks into me, her nose mashing into my back.

"Ow," she snaps.

I ignore her. Ruby does not feel pain like a normal human. Instead I look down at my feet. Although the X has long since been scuffed over, I know I'm in precisely the right spot.

"Looks like the band's coming on soon." Lauren reaches for the timetable and reads out the name. "SkyFires."

Where is he?

The stage goes as dark as possible at five-thirty in the height of summer and I turn to look out over the hushed crowd. Still no sign of him. A note is struck on the keyboard, a gently building tremble of sound that reaches out across the air, gathering strength when it's joined by an electric guitar.

Ruby nudges me just as a man's voice lifts up to join the rest of the sounds flowing from the speakers.

"Turn around."

I do as she says and my eyes go straight to the mic as the singer steps into the spotlight.

RUBY

This guy's presence is phenomenal. His *voice*... I let it sink into me and it's like the sound is speaking to my soul.

Beside me I feel Kaz blossom in the light from the stage. Like me, she's lost in the sensation of sound. Even Lauren, who never seems to shut up, has been stunned into the same silence as the rest of the crowd, held captive by a boy who can't be any older than Lee, who is not handsome, is not cool, but who is undeniably talented. We watch, listen, *feel* right to the last note of the first song before erupting into applause. I'm clapping so hard my skin stings and I'm screaming my support as if I'm the only person he can hear.

KAZ

The person onstage, the one whose voice has stolen every heart in here, is Sebastian. The boy I thought I was meeting is not one who stands in crowds, but one who stands on a stage. And it's a stage he *owns*.

"Hi. So we're SkyFires" – there's a swell of cheers and screams – "and this is our first festival."

Ruby wolf-whistles and Sebastian glances this way. He's wearing different clothes from before, but his glasses are the same – and his tousled hair. I wonder whether it feels as soft as it looks.

"This next one is about knowing what it means to escape."

Sebastian is a mesmerizing front man. Everything from the expressions he wears to the way he touches the mic with the tips of his fingers before throwing his arms wide and powering out the chorus draws the audience in. The rush of emotion has me smiling, eyes bright as I listen to him, my body tensed up on tiptoes, tilting towards him, straining to see him. His vocals give way to the guitar and he steps back from the mic before glancing this way.

Is he looking at me?

Don't be stupid, Kaz.

But he drew a cross on the ground…

And then he smiles and I *know* he's looking at me. Ruby's so immersed in the music that she's closed her eyes, whereas mine can barely keep away from the singer for more than a second.

"He's cute," Lauren whispers and I assume she must mean Sebastian, until she adds, "I never usually like the drummers."

Unlike Ruby, who *loves* a drummer.

I like a singer.

Or rather, I like *this* singer. When I look back, Sebastian's still looking at me and I can't help but smile. He ducks his head and rubs the back of his neck as the song draws to a close.

"So, how are we doing, guys? God, I'm shit at this frontman business," he says and everyone laughs. "I wrote a script and everything."

"He did," says the tall boy at the keyboard, surprising me because it seems as if Sebastian is the only person who should be onstage. "It was awful."

Everyone laughs again.

Sebastian takes control once more. "Maybe we should play another song?"

From next to me emerges a piercingly loud shout. "Yeah, you should!"

Sebastian glances this way, but this time it's not at me, but Ruby, who's smiling up at him, with her flirty, cheeky smile that has hooked every boy she's ever tried it on.

"Small person, big voice." He grins. "I guess I can identify with that."

And the band erupts into sound. Ruby turns to me, eyes sparkling with excitement.

"I can't believe he actually *spoke* to me!"

I want to tell her that I've spoken to him too, that the

reason we came here was … what? So I could fail to flirt with him? Or successfully flirt then fail to follow through?

Because I tried. I really did *try* to think about kissing Sebastian and all I ended up with was Tom. As if thinking about Sebastian is cheating on Tom, even though *he's* the one with the new girlfriend and *I'm* the free agent.

RUBY

When the set draws to a close, Kaz suggests we stay right where we are. Since I'm already prepped to try and sneak backstage to tell the band how amazing they are, staying put seems like a massive anti-climax. Although Lauren points out my chances of successfully clambering over the barrier aren't all that great and for once I can't disagree with her. The crowd shifts and thins as we look for signs of activity beyond the front of the stage. Most of it's panelled off, but you can see a few people moving around, setting up and sorting things out.

"So they were—" I start to say, but Lauren finishes for me: "Special."

Again, I find it hard to disagree. I don't like it.

"Yes," Kaz says, quietly. "That last track was…"

But there are no words to describe the enormity and the intimacy of their closing song. After today, I can't imagine how SkyFires won't become mega-huge famous rock stars. I'm so in love with their sound that I'm ready to tattoo their name across my heart.

"Hey." We turn to see the singer leaning on the barrier,

looking in our direction. I glance over my shoulder, but it seems he really is talking to us. "So, what did you make of the show?"

"Amazing." The word leaps out of my mouth before I can stop it, but he's looking at Kaz, who's just nodding, slowly.

"Out of ten?" he asks, which seems very bold.

"Nine," Kaz says, smiling at a point somewhere below his left nipple. "I'm marking it down a point for being too short."

Which is an excellent line. I'm proud of her. Although I wish she'd look up. She'll give the boy a complex.

"Sebastian," he says and reaches out a hand only for Lauren to be the first to snatch it.

"Lauren," she says. "And this is Kaz." There is a delightfully rude pause before she adds, "And Ruby."

At least she got my name right.

Sebastian isn't at all what I expected him to be. He's sweaty, for a start, which is hardly surprising, and he's changed out of the tight trousers and checked shirt he wore so well onstage, replacing them with tracksuit bottoms and a threadbare long-sleeved top that makes him look more like a prospector than a singer in a band. Those ugly-but-cool glasses he's wearing are performing a function, not a vanity, and close-to his face is lively, full of character, but it hasn't got the beauty it had from a distance. Until he smiles at something Kaz says, and it transforms him once more.

For the last year, Tom's beefy outdoorsy-ness cast

a shadow over Kaz's thing for boys who look like they prefer reading to rugby, but there was a time when she admitted to crushing on Callum – gross. This beautiful-on-the-inside boy has more than a whiff of the sensitive intellectual about him and I wonder if he's exactly what the Gods of Wounded Egos have ordered for my best friend...

"What are you three doing now?" he asks.

Kaz glances her question at Lauren, then me and I try to think of something witty.

"Er..." *Brain fail.*

Sebastian smiles at all three of us, although it's Kaz he directs the question to. "Do you fancy hanging out backstage with us?"

25 • BE CAREFUL WHAT
YOU ASK FOR

Backstage everything looks the same, only every element is suffused with a certain magic – a glamour in both senses of the word. The sun seems brighter, the people cleaner, the laughter louder. Flipping the lanyard over, I read the words GUEST PASS – SKYFIRES to reassure myself. Sebastian gave Lauren and me one each with Ruby picking the short straw and risking a broken wristband that she's pinned back together. Not that anyone here seems to care one way or the other. The only security I can see are driving quad bikes of people more important (or more lazy) than us through the crowds, and everyone else is too busy to worry about what anyone else is doing. We pass a group of girls consulting the schedule as one of them pulls out her phone. "I'm setting an alarm for eight forty-five. No way am I missing Gold'ntone."

When I look at my own phone, I'm dismayed at how little time that means we'll have with Sebastian.

Catching myself thinking this feels odd. It's been so long since I had a crush on anyone other than Tom that I'm not even sure that's what this is. Do I fancy him? Or do I just really like him?

It could be both…

Sebastian leads us to a table, where I recognize the other members of his band. He introduces everyone: Nick the drummer and Ferris, who I think was the tall keyboard player, and Eve, the bassist. Apparently their guitarist has gone for a nap in the back of their van.

"He always does that," Sebastian says to me. "Don't take it personally. Now, let me get this right." Sebastian points to Ruby first. "This is Ruby and Lauren. And this is Kaz."

My cheeks flush at the glance that Nick and Ferris exchange, but there's no time for awkwardness as Sebastian pulls over some spare chairs. Ruby sits down and shows no compunction in asking Nick if one of the beers is going spare. Something Lauren doesn't look too happy about.

"Drink?" Sebastian asks.

"Is there any water?" I can only see beer.

"I'll get you some." And he stands to leave. My dismay must show, because he asks if I want to go with him.

Which I do.

"So. Er…" I walk with him to the bar, hoping to strike flirtatious gold.

"How's your day been?" Sebastian asks.

"Nice." I'm useless at this.

"That's a very vague word."

"I know. Sorry." The queue for the bar here is tiny compared to the arena – only two-people deep.

"Why say sorry?" Sebastian smiles into my eyes. "Vague is permitted."

"OK. How about your day?"

"Mostly fine, escalating to exquisitely nerve-wracking."

I can imagine why. "You didn't need to be nervous – that set was amazing. *You* were amazing." And then because this sounds a bit over the top, I panic and add, "Your band were amazing."

"Don't let them know you called them 'my' band," Sebastian says in a whisper that's quiet enough for him to lean in.

"Well, SkyFires are amazing, then."

"Oh, I know that." His somewhat goofy grin dilutes the arrogance of the statement. "I'm not a fan of fake modesty. I like the music we make – we can draw in a good crowd and we've interest from someone who wants to manage us. We play to bigger crowds in our hometown than here." Sebastian glances at me and then away, shuffling forwards towards the bar. "That wasn't what I was nervous about."

Performing here would still make me nervous, but… "What were you nervous about, then?"

"Just a girl I met."

"Oh," I say, disappointed.

But Sebastian ducks his head, forcing me to meet his eyes. "That girl is you."

"Oh." This time I do not sound evenly faintly disappointed. "Now you've made *me* nervous."

His laugh is uncomplicated and happy. "You've no need to be. I'm not after anything sinister, just your company."

"Really?"

Sebastian nods. "So far I'm enjoying it a lot."

And even though I'm smiling mostly at the grass between his feet, when I glance up, he's looking at me as if that really is what he wants from me.

"Water?" he asks and I nod.

I definitely have a crush.

RUBY

I'm tired of having Lauren cock-block me every time I try to talk to Drummer Boy Nick. Really fucking irritating when all I want to do is find out more about Sebastian ON KAZ'S BEHALF. Also, really fucking pointless. Lauren's a one-focus kind of girl, so she hasn't noticed that Nick and Eve are totally a couple. One of those really relaxed ones that are so comfortable in their togetherness that they don't need to advertise it beyond the familiarity of a hand-touch here or a secret smile there.

When I say I'm going to the loo, Lauren shuffles in closer to Nick and I smile at Eve, who winks at me. I guess if you're in a band with your boyfriend you get used to it.

The toilets here have had a lot less use than the ones in the main arena. They're like the ones down by the main stage: Portakabins complete with sinks, although these ones have functioning soap dispensers and actual toilet roll. There are a couple of girls in there, talking about having to take a picture to go with their write-up of the afternoon's gossip. The one with the plumage of a tropical bird plaited into her hair accosts me at the sink, accusing my outfit of being totally grunge-punk chic and cooing over my arm – "Is it real?" – not waiting for an answer as she loops an arm around me and hauls me outside, asking if she can take a photo.

Before I can really decide whether I want that, the deed is done and Feather Head's friend/colleague, whose necklace looks like a pterodactyl clinging to the cliff-face of her collarbone, is asking me whether I'm eighteen.

Given that I'm planning on heading barwards at some point, I sneer slightly and say, "Thanks a lot!" as if I'm massively insulted that she'd even ask.

Necklace Girl holds the phone steady as she asks, "What's your name, how old are you and do you mind if we post your picture as part of the festival fashion piece for *Gozzip Magazine*?"

"Ruby Kalinski. Er, eighteen. No, sure, use my picture however you want."

They tell me I'm done, but as they faff finding the right filter or whatever, Feather Head tells me to keep an eye on the Festblog feed. "A few of these street-style snaps go up there."

Ugh. Festblog. Maybe I was a little hasty giving permission, but it's too late now – my hyperactive photographers have already started walking off. Besides, what's the worst that could happen? I didn't have my arse hanging out or anything and it's not like I'm Megan Mallory or someone actually famous.

Kaz is back at the table, but before I get there, I see Lauren laughing, resting her arm on my mate's shoulder; my feet slow to a stop and I can't seem to get them going again. At least, not in that direction.

At the bar, it dawns on me that no one in here will believe my lie about being eighteen. The women look *magnificent* – they're all seven-foot tall and wearing lipstick, both of which automatically make you look older. Standing on my tiptoes and swiping on some

Vaseline is not going to cut it. Or grease it.

I turn back and walk straight into someone holding a full pint.

"Shit!" I'm not sure which of us said it the loudest.

"I'm so sorry – can I get you another one? Only, I don't think I'll get served and I don't have my ID on me, so could you…?"

My voice trails off when I realize who I'm gibbering at Kaz-style.

Adam Wexler stops angry-frowning and starts thinking-frowning.

"I asked you to sign my belt," I say. Then I point helpfully to my crotch. Awesome.

"The girl with the ex-boyfriend."

"Could be anyone, that, couldn't it?" I say.

"But it's you I'm talking to." He touches my shoulder, gently turning me towards the bar and guiding me forwards. I do my best not to faint. "How about we procure a drink and you tell me how successful you've been at getting your own back?"

"Well, I've not revenge-snogged anyone yet," I say, trying to hold my nerve.

Wexler lowers his head so that his mouth is next to my ear as we approach the bar.

"*Yet,*" he says, quietly, leaning away to order two beers.

KAZ

The band are funny, especially Nick, who is fantastic at

impressions and is currently circling the picnic table in a perfect "Moves Like Jagger" dance, leaving all of us in stitches. The others start begging him to do an impression of Adam Wexler and I glance at my phone to find there's a message from Ruby.

Have found a hot boy. Will come find you before GT. K? X

I message back. *Picture?*

She resends the Adam Wexler photo she found on Tumblr.

I meant a picture of the one you're with, idiot.

Be patient. You'll see him later anyway. Hope you're making good progress with S.

My eyes slide to meet Sebastian's and my heart accelerates to triple time. There isn't much time between now and when we'll need to leave to join the crowd for Gold'ntone – we need to get in early if we want to make it to the front before they come onstage.

"Do you want to come and watch Gold'ntone with us?" I ask, edging closer, not wanting to discuss this with all the others as well.

"So you're a Gold'ntone fan, then?" Sebastian doesn't quite answer my question and I get cold feet that maybe he doesn't like them and somehow I'm horribly uncool, which is why I answer only half truthfully.

"Not as much as Ruby."

"Your other friend." He nods, looking round for her, even though she's not here for him to see. It feels odd to have Ruby referred to as "other".

"Ruby and I came here together. She's my best friend."

Sebastian looks at Lauren and raises his eyebrows in question. "Lauren is … new to the group."

His focus sharpens. "You seem like you've known each other a while."

I laugh at this, a little embarrassed about how short that while actually is. "She's going out with one of my friends."

"*Boy* friend or *girl* friend?"

"Ex-boyfriend, actually." Sebastian watches me, but I don't know what it is that he's thinking and I look away as I add, "You're thinking that's pretty weird, I suppose."

"I'm thinking that *you're* pretty, Kaz." And I glance up to see him studying me. "That's all I was thinking."

He still hasn't answered my question about Gold'ntone.

RUBY

Our cups are empty.

"Your shout, Ruby." Wexler nudges my foot with his toe.

"Yeah … about that…"

"You're not eighteen, are you?" Wexler leans in, one elbow resting on the table, his face not far from mine. Breathing is very difficult, but I try not to act too flustered. It's the first time he's asked a serious question, and I guess it's the kind that needs a serious answer.

"More like sixteen." I concentrate on holding his gaze, making sure he knows I'm old enough to handle another beer. And myself.

"You know you're staring?" Wexler says in a voice that I have to inch closer to hear.

"You know you're an incredibly famous rock star?" I whisper back. "Staring is kind of the law."

Wexler laughs then, leaning back in his chair, looking at me as if I'm something he was surprised to find. Or maybe it's a move. I've had a lot of practice playing this kind of game with Stu, but he was my equal. Wexler is not, in any way shape or form, my equal.

But he does appear to be playing down at my level. For now. "Is that all I am to you? An *incredibly* famous rock star?"

It's clear he's mocking himself, not me.

"Are you meant to be anything else?"

"I thought we were bonding here. Becoming friends. Exchanging revenge stories, revealing devastating ways we've broken hearts…"

"I think you might have broken more than me," I say.

Wexler narrows his eyes and I see a flash of white as he bites his lower lip. His eyes are so piercing it's as if he's looking right into my fantasies.

"It's quality, Ruby, not quantity." Then he goes to get up, pausing as he stoops near. "And something tells me you're quality through and through." He stays close, letting me hear him breathe. I'm aware that his mouth is getting closer to my ear and then he gives my earlobe not a kiss but a gentle pinch of teeth and a light tug. A fraction of a second later, he flashes me an entirely wicked grin that makes my insides quiver as he gets up to go to the bar. "We've time for one more…"

Once I'm alone, I hold my hand out flat. Or at least

I try to – it's more than a little bit shaky. As is the rest of me.

I can't believe this is happening. He is *so very sexy*.

Watching him come back with two pints of beer, my heart plummets between my legs and thumps there insistently. Wexler puts the drinks down and runs a finger along my wrist as if getting my attention, then presses my unspent tenner into my palm.

"My stage call's in fifteen minutes." *How is that the time?* "No one's allowed stage-side."

As if I thought that was on the cards. A nibble on the earlobe might be five-star flirting, but it's not a promotion from fan to entourage.

"I'll be fine watching the normal way, at the front of the stage," I say.

Wexler drinks some of his beer. I drink some of mine. I'm feeling a little woozy. I drink some more.

"So you won't be coming backstage afterwards?" he asks.

I drink again, because it's easier than using actual words when he's looking at me like that.

"Because I'd like it if you were." *Seriously, is this actually happening?* "I feel like I'm the one doing all the talking here."

And he comes closer, moving his chair forwards until his leg is between mine, his face filling my vision with his sexy eyes and lips.

And then I lose my mind, because I, Ruby Kalinski, go in for a kiss. WITH ADAM FUCKING WEXLER.

26 • FIND MY WAY BACK

RUBY

I feel like one of those wooden donkeys with tubes for legs held straight by taut strings that collapse when you press a button. Taut, loose, taut, loose. If I wasn't concentrating so hard on walking, I'd probably slide sideways and fall right over.

That last beer hit me hard. Or that kiss.

I can't work out which I find harder to believe: that I went in for a snog with a rock god or that he actually kissed me back.

Adam Wexler. Kissed me.

Suddenly my legs are very loose and I have to stop for a second.

With tongues.

Now my whole body appears to have gone floppy.

Such a hot kiss.

It barely seems real given how many times I've fantasized about it, but I suck my bottom lip into my mouth and run my tongue across the most tender part, where his tooth scored the skin.

Definitely real.

I've come over all fuggy. Beer? Sunshine? Lust?

My brain is incapable of sensible thought. My mouth incapable of sensible action.

I am all over incapable of sensible anything.

But then I've never been the sensible one.

I need to find Kaz...

KAZ

"Where's Ruby?" Lauren asks when I tell her it's time to go. "I thought Gold'ntone was going to be the highlight of her year?"

When we tell the others where we're going, Ferris rolls his eyes and Nick comes out with, "Blinded by your vaginas, like everyone else." Which earns him a punch on the arm from Eve.

"Don't be a dick." Eve smiles at me. "Some men feel threatened by hotness."

"Who says I'm threatened?" Nick looks outraged. "I know I'm hot. I wouldn't have landed a girl as gorgeous as you otherwise."

He puts an arm around Eve and kisses her cheek, his nose mashing into the side of her head as she tries to push him off. Lauren looks uncomfortable about this – whatever she feels for Tom, it hasn't stopped her attention from wandering – first Stu, now Nick... Guilt punches me in the lungs and I'm winded by my own hypocrisy.

"I take it you guys are staying here, then?" Sebastian says, sliding off the table to stand next to me. Another of those glances pass between Nick and Ferris, and Eve tells him they're going to wake the guitarist and catch the band headlining the Mellow Tent later.

"We'll see you by the van at midnight if we don't hear from you before." This time it's Eve who's giving me a funny look and I feel myself burning up under the scrutiny. As Sebastian nods his agreement, Eve reaches over to give me a hug. "It was nice to meet you," she says, before halving the volume to add, "He likes you. This doesn't happen often, so be gentle with him."

It's exactly the sort of thing that Ruby would say to Sebastian.

Where is she?

I call her on our way to the exit.

"Where are you?" I say.

"Bins."

"Which bins?" *And why?*

"Ones opposite the bar, near the gate."

I tap Lauren on the arm and point in that direction, before brushing my fingers down Sebastian's arm to guide him. Or just as an excuse to touch him.

Still on the phone to Ruby, I say, "We're heading over. Are you OK?"

"Not sure."

"What about this hot boy you promised me?"

"Not sure."

"Are you drunk?"

"Not sure."

"For God's sake, Ruby!" I'm not in the mood for cryptic. She's been awkward all day and I've run out of patience ... and that's when I see her, leaning heavily on an overflowing bin. She's resting her head on one hand, holding the phone to her face with the other, even though I've just hung up.

Lauren's seen her too. "Is Ruby drunk?"

Lauren's mouth is open, eyebrows puckered together in a perfect depiction of what Ruby would call Scandalized Face. For the first time today, I suspect that Ruby's right to think that Lauren doesn't like her – although after last night, I'm hardly enamoured of Drunk Ruby either.

"Not sure," I say to Lauren.

RUBY

We plunge into the crowd together, me at the front of our little snake, Lauren following, Kaz behind her with Sebastian. I asked where the rest of the band went, but now I can't remember what the answer was. I push forwards, careless of the people I'm trampling in my haste.

The first thing Kaz said was, "You're drunk." Which I probably am but is not the point.

And then Lauren asked me where my fabled hot boy was.

Fabled.

"I sent Kaz a photo."

Lauren laughed a "HA!" with such a sharp little yap that it made me wince. Then Kaz told me it didn't matter and that we'd be late for Gold'ntone, and the beautiful-but-not Sebastian was looking at me like I was something to pity and I couldn't bear it...

"Wait up, Ruby!" Lauren catches hold of my sleeve and I yank it from her grasp.

"Don't touch me!" I yell, loud enough that Kaz and Sebastian and the twenty people crushed into a two-metre radius hear me.

"No need to bite my head off!" Lauren looks offended and Kaz puts a comforting hand on her shoulder.

"Ruby…" It's her telling-me-off voice. Kaz has decided that I am drunk and everything I do from now on is entirely unreasonable.

I HAVEN'T EVEN DRUNK THAT MUCH.

I probably HAVEN'T EVEN DRUNK THAT MUCH.

Kaz is supposed to be the person I can trust to see straight through all my bullshit. When did the pair of us get so fucking blind that we couldn't even read the truth in each other?

I turn away. "I want to get closer."

As I storm on, ignoring the tuts and squeals and "watch where you're going"s, I bump my chin on someone's elbow and bite through the sore spot on my lip. The pain is sharp and welcome and sobering, but it doesn't last long enough to distract me from how upset I am about Kaz.

The only other thing to think about is the band. The music. The man making it.

It's stupid in a crowd this size to hope that he'll find me, but I don't stop until we're as near to the stage as we're likely to get.

"Ruby!" Lauren holds me back as a bottle of suspiciously yellow fluid flies from above and plummets to the ground. The pissile explodes, but I'm clear.

"We should move further back," Lauren's saying to Kaz, who's nodding.

"It's a pretty intense crowd," adds Sebastian. But Kaz looks at me and I forget that I'm hurt, because my best friend is not immediately doing whatever pleases Lauren.

"I don't want to move," I say, cheek pressed against the back of the girl in front as the crowd lifts me off my feet.

"OK." I hear Kaz loud and clear because the crowd has moved her closer. "But if I faint, promise me you'll illegally crowd-surf me out of here?"

I squeeze her hand by way of a promise since my mouth is full of someone else's hair.

When the stage lights flare, most of the band burst on, creating a space around the microphone at the front of the stage, waiting for the heart of the band to start beating. Mine *thud thuds* in time with the bass drum. The second he steps into the spotlight, the crowd heaves amidst a swell of screams. Wexler is wearing a suit jacket, the vest underneath cut low enough to show off the new tattoo we've all been speculating about. The possibility of seeing more of it if I go backstage superheats my core and I start trembling.

I want to tell Kaz, but I don't think it's the wisest thing to shout that I've snogged Adam Wexler in the midst of some girls wearing tees with "I want to sex the Wex" scrawled in lipstick. Or blood.

"Ruby!" Kaz is yanking at my hand. "It's our song!"

And she throws our arms in the air, squeezing my hand

tight as I jump and scream in joy when the familiar chords sound out. I look up to see our hands locked together above the crowd, silhouetted against the stage lights.

KAZ

Ruby running up the stairs into my room shouting, "Listen to this, listen to this!" jamming one of her headphones into my ear so hard that I fell off my chair.

The email I got on my phone with the subject PLAY ME NOW! and clicking through to the video when it only had 73 views.

Dancing round the classroom in a conga when it came on the radio one lunchtime.

The print Ruby made of my favourite lyric that she had framed for my birthday. The tears I cried because she knew me so well.

Friday nights by the DJ booth, putting in at least twenty requests for this song, giggling too hard to write the words properly on the Post-its.

The "Kaz, Kaz, Kaz!" when it came on the playlist in Owen's van on the way here – the marks on my leg after she'd gripped it in excitement at the thought of seeing them tonight.

I'm squeezing Ruby's hand tighter with each memory, until her fingers are half-crushed. Music has made me cry for the love of it before, but now I feel like crying for the love of my best friend. My crazy, jealous, moody (possibly drunk) best friend who I love more than anyone else in the world.

More than I ever loved Tom. More than I could ever love Lauren.

"Everything Ends Midnight" – but not tonight.

Not me and Ruby.

27 • MAYDAY [M'AIDEZ]

RUBY

Seven songs in and they've got to be near to closing the set. As if on cue, Wexler, now jacketless, ribbed vest clinging to his body, tells us that this is the last song. His gaze sweeps the audience, as it has so many times already, and I imagine that he's looking for me, when I know he's really just seeking adoration. I stare at the stage, hoping, dreaming that this time he will see me.

Just as it seems he won't, his eyes rest on my patch of the crowd.

And he points.

"For revenge," he says into the microphone. The breath whooshes from my lungs like I've been punched in the chest as he sings the song the crowd's been waiting for. *"When a kiss becomes a knife…"*

My blood floods hot with excitement: I really, actually am going to do this, aren't I?

When this song finishes, when the band leave the stage, I will use my fake pass and I will find Adam Wexler backstage.

And then…

At the thought of what happens next all that hot blood is redirected to a less-than-vital organ. It's certainly drained right out of my brain because even though I'll get mobbed if anyone hears me, I'm turning to Kaz, desperate to tell her and I'm opening my mouth, finding the words…

But she's gone. The girl at my shoulder is not my best friend. She's not even someone I know. I look desperately around, but Kaz is nowhere to be seen. I start pushing against the people behind me, burrowing under their raised arms, slipping through gaps between bodies and standing on tiptoes, desperate to catch sight of Kaz or Sebastian – even Lauren.

Kaz has gone. Left me. Abandoned me when I needed her most, because she is the person I tell when I want things to be real. She *makes* them real…

Right now the only thing made real is my fear that I have lost her to Lauren.

KAZ

How did it happen? Where's Ruby? She was there a second ago and now I can't find her. I'm panicking, trying to push through the crowd back to where I think she'll be, but when I get there she isn't anywhere to be seen. I try to line myself up with the stage. We were right below Adam Wexler, who's reaching out towards the crowd, even though the barriers have us penned so far back he'd have to turn into Mr Tickle to stand a chance of reaching us.

He looks almost *dangerous* – preying on the crowd's adulation to feed his ego. Stripped back to his vest, his muscles stand out as he puts everything into his performance.

His eyes are wild. Savage. And he's sexier than ever. I think of him whispering in my ear at the signing tent.

Enjoy the show.

I felt so special when he said it. No doubt so did all the other girls who are here now, desperate for him to notice them…

"Kaz!" There's a shout from behind me, but it's only Lauren, pulling me back, away from where I think Ruby will be. I don't want to go, but Lauren looks frightened and when I reach her, Sebastian's there too, saying we should go — Lauren's breathing really fast as if she might faint. We get to where the crowd thins out as the music fades and the band wave, before stepping offstage to deafening cheers. The sinking sun casts a golden light across the heads and hands of the crowd, dust clouds puffing up as everyone starts to shift, and I worry about little Ruby, lost amongst them.

RUBY

"Excuse me, love. Can I see your pass, please?"

Crap.

I hold out my wrist and the security guard clocks the safety pin immediately.

"Back out into the main arena, please."

I open my mouth to say something, but nothing comes out.

"Go on. You're not the first and you won't be the last." The guard holds out an arm, shepherding me like I'm a lost little lamb separated from the herd in the arena, but as I'm about to turn away, someone steps out of the flow of people coming back from the stage.

"Is there a problem here?"

Frozen, I watch as Wexler fixes the festival guy with a look. There's an energy about him that wasn't there earlier and it's both scary and seductive.

"This young lady hasn't got permission to be back here."

"She's with me."

The security guard looks at Wexler for an unimpressed second, then back at me. "You're with this guy?"

"Hell, yeah," I mutter, because that guy is just about the most terrifyingly sexy human my eyes have ever seen. Saying nothing, Wexler guides me round a couple of tents, past the bar and into a dead end behind a cluster of cabins. The tension inside me twists tighter and tighter until I think I'm going to be sick if I don't release it.

He's wired, high from his performance, and there's a dangerous edge to him now that I didn't see earlier. Leaning in, his fingers latching on to the grille of the barrier behind me, he brings his face level with mine. I can hear him breathing, fast and deep to match the pulse in my throat.

The tension in the air between us would be enough to get me off, but already he's drawing closer and I'm riding the moments towards our kiss like they're the last of my life.

Worried as I was about Ruby, whatever's wrong with Lauren seemed more pressing and I didn't have a chance to do anything more than fire off a message to Ruby, telling her that we were heading for the first-aid tent.

Even as I sent it, I couldn't help feeling like I'd betrayed my best friend. Our moment in the crowd was more than a fleeting happiness: it was a reminder of why I'm here and who I'm with. This weekend has made me doubt whether Ruby and I have the perfect friendship, but I see now that I haven't always been the perfect friend. Perhaps Ruby's behaviour has been the worst I've ever seen because that's how she *feels*? Something I haven't taken the time to ask her about … not properly.

Once Lauren is with a St John Ambulance official, who's making her breathe into a paper bag, I check my phone for a reply from Ruby to discover that my message never sent.

I send it again and wait for a reply.

There isn't one.

RUBY

When Wexler's mouth is next to mine, it's a question I get, not a kiss. "Are you sure, Ruby?"

Saying nothing, I pull him towards me. This doesn't feel like a kiss, more like sex with my mouth, and I'm aware of the heel of his hand against my ear, his fingers massaging the hair at the back of my head, thumb pressing into my temple.

When I pull away to catch my breath, his pupils are huge, as if his eyes can't get enough of me, and I feel a surge of pride, of power, that I'm the one doing this to him. That *I* am the one he wants.

It's a dangerous feeling.

KAZ

The St John's lady tells Lauren she'd be best off having a rest and Lauren doesn't argue, but I'm frustrated that we'll have to walk her back to the tent and put off looking for Ruby. Her phone keeps going straight to voicemail.

Sebastian rests a hand on my arm. "I'm sure your friend's fine."

I want to correct him – *best* friend – but I don't. Neither Ruby nor I have been at our best this weekend.

And I am not sure that she's fine.

RUBY

Wexler has brought me back to the "van" – a term I took too literally. The thing he's leading me towards is not a van – it's a fucking *house*. Admittedly, one with wheels.

"What are you waiting for?" Wexler looks around, confused as to why I'm still standing on the grass, as if I'm not playing the part I'm supposed to. It makes me wonder what kind of reaction he was expecting.

A bubble of doubt spirals up from the depths of my thoughts: *I've never had sex with someone I wasn't going out with.*

But as soon as it hits the surface, it pops and the feeling's gone.

"I'm waiting for you to lead the way," I say and take a step after him onto the bus.

28 • IN MOTION

RUBY

There are a lot of people in here. Too many. I find myself pressed into a corner, clutching a bottle of beer in each fist, watching as the band laugh and shout and flirt with girls older than me – the seven-foot tall ones with loads of make-up and an air of experience about them. When I walked in, the guitarist called out, "Belt Girl!" and handed me bottles from the bucket next to him.

"I see you've already made friends with Marc," Wexler said. "He only gives beer to the pretty ones."

I'd held up my two bottles and said quietly enough that Marc wouldn't hear, "I'm glad he's so shallow."

Before I could lean away again, Wexler held me back. "I'm glad he's not the one you're here with."

It might have been a compliment, but it left me feeling a bit weird, like there's a chance Marc could ever have had me, like I'm a prize and not a person... I find I've drunk one of the bottles already, but since I don't know where to put it, I just hold on to it whilst sipping nervously at the other. Before he could sit down with me, Wexler got sidetracked by someone I don't know – their manager, I guess, since he looks way older than everyone else. They're obviously talking about something to do with me and I watch the man glance over at me as Wexler says, "Don't worry, it's fine."

I don't think he knows I'm listening, but Manager Man does. "It's not," he says, pulling Wexler further down the bus.

The leather of the seat pinches at the back of my knees as I shift my weight.

My second beer is gone.

The tide of lust that swept me ashore is drawing back in Wexler's absence. I peel the labels off the bottles and roll the paper into thin tubes before I notice I'm being stared at. It's one of the girls sitting at the table with the guitarist. She doesn't turn away when she sees me looking, but gets up and comes over.

"Shift up," she says and I obey, aware of the bare skin of this stranger's leg pressing against mine as we squash onto the seat. "I'm Kaya."

"Ruby." My voice sounds as small as I feel next to this goddess. She smells like expensive perfume and her hair is smooth and shiny – as is her skin.

"So you're with Adam?"

I nod.

"How old are you?"

"Eighteen," I lie automatically.

"I mean how old are you now, not how old are you in three years' time."

I smile a thin smile and tell the truth. "I'm sixteen." Kaya looks like she doesn't believe me. "I'm telling the truth."

Kaya lays a hand on my thigh as she leans closer. "I'm only looking out for you, sweetie. Are you sure you know what you're doing?" Her eyes are accented by perfectly applied liner and her lashes are so long I'm sure they can't be real. She is much more beautiful than me. Much more worldly. "Look. Go and get some air. Clear your head. This might not be the right scene for someone like you."

Presumably it is for someone like her. "Are you his girlfriend or something?"

Kaya throws her head back and laughs, making me feel even smaller. "Adam only sleeps with people prepared to worship him. I don't worship anyone." As she stops laughing, she stares at me. "But you do, don't you?"

I don't know what to say to this.

Kaya plucks the empty bottles from my hands and nods towards the other end of the bus. "Take a breather. You can always come back if this is what you want."

Doing as I'm told, I stand up too quickly, then nearly fall over as I try to step over the tangle of legs stretched out across the width of the tour bus, like I'm playing a game of ladders in the school hall. The guitarist – Marc – stands up in front of me and declares he's going to the toilet. He waves a little plastic bag at the people at the table.

"Want to join me, Belt Girl?" He's smiling a little intensely and I realize this probably isn't his first trip there.

"I…" I've no experience of turning down hardcore drugs. No one has ever offered me anything stronger than a bit of weed. "No, thanks, I'm fine for the, um …" – this is painful – "… drugs. Thanks for offering. It was, er, nice of you."

The table behind me erupts into laughter.

I hurry towards the end of the bus and the exit – I can almost taste my relief as I get there…

"Ruby?" Adam Wexler is on the step below me, his face level with mine, hands clamped around the rails, arms stretching across the width of the exit. "You OK?"

No. "Yes. Just need a bit of air."

"Those guys can be a bit much. I'm sorry I left you. PR emergency."

There's no sign of Manager Man.

"Is your emergency over, then?"

He stares at me for a moment. "It's just getting started…" And he kisses me. It's less urgent, less adult than our last kiss, but when I kiss him a little harder, he responds and my confidence grows. This is something I know how to do.

When he breaks away I feel drunk, as if Wexler's kiss contained five times more alcohol than those beers. He runs his hands under my vest and it's hard not to think of Stu's hands doing the same…

How I'd feel less on edge if it was.

"Everything all right?"

I nod quickly. I don't want Wexler to be Stu – that's kind of the point.

"Come on," he murmurs, slipping his hand in mine, guiding me back inside the bus towards a door I assumed was a toilet.

It is not a toilet.

I shut the door behind me and lean against it, my legs a little wobbly at the sight of what's inside. A bed. And Adam Wexler: the man I've dreamed about, whose lyrics I've cried to, whose voice I've sung along to, whose eyes have looked out at me from a thousand different pictures in magazines and online.

I am not entirely sure how I got here, but Past Ruby would totally be high-fiving Present Ruby right about now.

Hooking a finger in the belt he signed, Wexler pulls me gently towards him, then he leans forward and kisses my cheek, murmuring in my ear, *"If I sang you a song …"*

It's the start of "Tonight Too Soon" – my favourite song.

"… filled with loving and longing …"

This feels like a line, but the way he's kissing my neck and …

"… you would give yourself over …"

… pushing aside the strap of my vest and my bra to kiss my shoulder.

"… to want and belonging …"

He pulls off my vest to kiss my collarbone and reaches down.

"… I want what you've got …"

And unclicks the clasp.

"… and I get what I want …"

To kiss the bare skin of my breasts.

"… so give in to me now …"

I take a step back, falling onto the mattress of the bed behind and pulling him down on top of me. I am in this.

"… because I want …" A kiss. *"… want …"* Nip. *"… want…"* Bite.

And as I part my lips for another kiss, I do not let myself consider that this might not be what I want, want, want.

Because I *do* want this.

Don't I?

KAZ

It almost comes as a shock to find Roly back at the camp with Stella and her friends. I was starting to think he'd left completely. There's no sign of Tom and Naj, which is a relief.

I make Roly promise to stay near in case Lauren needs help and I give her a hug goodbye, aware that Roly's surprise at seeing us together has risen an octave into shock.

He had every chance to tell me the truth yesterday and he didn't.

I don't like Roly. I don't like Naj.

I don't even know whether I like Tom any more.

I like Lauren though.

And I like Sebastian, who is nothing like Tom in any way shape or form, but I don't want him to be. Every word he's said to me has been kind, and as we amble back along the path, after we pass a man sitting in the middle of the path wearing a T-shirt on his head, Sebastian pulls me to a stop.

I think that he's going to kiss me, but what he actually does is a thousand times more romantic than that.

"Do you want to try looking for your friend?" Sebastian asks.

It makes me want to wrap my arms around him and never let him go.

Whilst I try Ruby again, Sebastian calls his friends,

but Ferris, who's backstage packing up, says he's not seen her and when we get to our camp it's empty, tents zipped up tight, fire cold. I go in and check for Ruby in the tent anyway, just in case.

When I come back out, Sebastian's talking to some-one – Owen.

"Have you seen Ruby?" I ask right away, but he shakes his head.

"Your friend already asked."

"Do you think she's with Lee and the others?"

"What makes you think I know where Lee is?" Owen's voice is sharp.

"You're his—" But the look he gives me strangles the meaning out of my sentence. "I'll call him."

"Don't bother. Wherever he is, he's not with Ruby." Then he sucks in a breath and the change in his voice is as if he's flipped to a new song sheet. "I'm heading back to the arena, just came to grab some stuff."

His hands are empty.

"Which band are you seeing?" I ask.

"Three Letter Acronym." The Heavy Tent headliners. Owen offers to look for Ruby in the crowd before giving me an all-encompassing hug and telling me that the Kalinskis are a tough bunch and Ruby's the toughest of the lot. "She'll be fine, Kaz. The girl's made of Teflon."

Everyone seems so convinced that Ruby's fine and yet I can't shake the feeling that she isn't.

Once Owen's gone, Sebastian reaches over and pulls me closer to him.

"Is there anywhere else you want to look?" His fingers are calloused against my palm and without thinking, I turn his over to stroke the tough skin on his fingers and he laughs. "The price of playing too much guitar."

"I figured. I play too — not as much, obviously." I turn my hand over and he mirrors the way I touched his.

It feels a lot like he might be about to kiss me...

"Coffee!" I shout in his face, then start walking backwards until my foot catches in a pothole and I collapse to the ground.

My ankle hurts.

Twenty minutes later and it still hurts, but at least I have the coffee I was so keen on. And Sebastian, on whom I am also keen. We're sitting up by the line of trees that stand guard across the highest hill of the campsite, the field below a constellation of campfires. Even though we can hear the cheers of a crowd we can't see and the catcalls tossed between the campers, the world feels peaceful, muted.

In this subdued bubble, I can hear Sebastian sip and swallow.

"I like it here," he says.

"Here on the hill? Here at the festival?"

"Here. In this moment. In this place." Everything he says makes me want to smile. "I'll probably use that in a song."

He sips his tea again and waggles his eyebrows, making me laugh.

"Nothing's sacred?"

"Not to a songwriter. Words, thoughts, feelings —

everything I see or hear or touch. All a song to be written."

He's beautiful. Not specifically to look at, but to be with.

Sebastian's looking at me carefully and I can see the subtle twitch in his eyes as he studies my face before meeting my gaze. The world recedes so far that there's only me and him sitting alone on a hill in a field that only exists for us to sit there. He puts his cup down in the grass and then brushes a thumb across my cheek, pulling back to show me the eyelash he's captured.

"I've stolen a wish," he says.

"Not stolen," I reply. "Saved."

"Very poetic. I'll steal – sorry, *save* – that too."

The eyelash is still resting in the whorl of his thumbprint, waiting for one of us to claim it.

"I'll let you have it," I say over the rim of my cup. "I'm generous like that."

Sebastian closes his eyes and blows my eyelash away across the field, his lips curved in a smile so private I'm almost embarrassed to have noticed it.

I think I know what he wished for.

I think it's what I would have wished for too…

I am going to kiss this boy who isn't Tom and I am going to do it now.

Only what I actually do is headbutt Sebastian in the nose as he reaches for his tea, knocking the glasses from his face.

"Oh my God, I am so sorry!" I say. For a second I think he's crying until I realize it's laughter.

"I'm fine. It's fine. My nose is fine. You really don't need to apologize." But the fact that he checks his hand for blood when he lifts it away is far from reassuring. (Although there doesn't appear to be any.)

Replacing his glasses, he says, "Do you want to try that again?" He edges forward slowly to place a soft, cool kiss on my lips.

A slight hesitation and I kiss him back, lips pressing briefly before I withdraw.

That was nice.

But Sebastian reaches out, his fingers running along the bumps of my braids, along the edge of my ear to rest lightly on my jaw.

"Again," he whispers and this time, the kiss isn't so soft – but it's just as nice.

We stay like that, sitting, kissing in our bubble on the hill until we eventually have to stop. I'm cold and the other members of SkyFires keep calling to find out where their designated tour van driver has gone.

"I could stay," Sebastian says, kissing my cheek, then the lobe of my ear and my jaw.

I smile as I say, "No. You couldn't."

"You're right. I can't – my friends would kill me." He stands up, pulling me with him until my lips reach his once more and I breathe him in. He smells like his songs.

When I pull back I feel giddy.

"Are we going to do this again?" Sebastian asks as he slides his hand into mine. Our fingers intertwine the way I always wanted to do with Tom and never did.

"Same time next year?" I'm making light of it, because I don't know how else to handle it.

"That's a long time to wait between kisses." Sebastian turns me to him and we stop on the path amidst a stream of people flowing from the arena.

"About two minutes and fifteen seconds, sixteen seconds…" I'm still talking as I press my lips to his and we smile through another kiss. And then another, until a passerby shouts, "Disgusting! That's what tents are for, mate!"

And I pull away, hot with humiliation, my mind full of thoughts of Mum's condoms and the horror of actually having a reason to use any of them.

"Out in the open is fine for me." Sebastian squeezes my hand.

"Me too." But my mind's moved on to what I *have* done in the privacy of a tent – how much has happened since then and what will happen next…

"I really do have to go, Kaz." Sebastian kisses my cheek. "Although I wish I didn't. What's your number? Your email? Your address? Anything?"

Much as I want this to happen again, I worry that it can't – not the way I'd like it to. Not until I'm free from Tom. For the first time today, Sebastian looks something other than confident as I refrain from answering his question. "You know I'm not someone who usually goes round plucking beautiful girls from the audience and kissing them, don't you?"

I can't help but smile. "Did you just call me beautiful?"

"You are."

Tom never once called me beautiful.

And it's the fact that I can't get him out of my head that's stopping me from handing over my number. I don't want to be like Tom, messing up my next relationship because I haven't recovered from the last. If I see Sebastian again, I want it to be because I want to be with *him*, not because I can't be alone.

It is not Sebastian's job to cure me of Tom. It's mine. And for that I need time.

"How about I find you?" I say.

"That sounds sinister," Sebastian says, but I kiss his joke away.

"SkyFires must have a website?" He nods. "With a contact form?" Another nod. "That someone regularly checks?"

"That someone would be me."

I kiss him again. "Then that makes finding you when the time is right easy, doesn't it?"

"When the time is right?"

This time it's me who nods, perhaps with a little more certainty than I feel.

"I hope that time is soon," Sebastian says.

30 • DARK BLUE

RUBY

I hurry off the bus, nearly tripping over my boots because I haven't put them on properly. I stop, hand resting on the bonnet to balance as I kick my toes down into the ends. Could do without a broken ankle. Then I half run, half hobble, because I still haven't done up my laces, as fast as I can away from there, away from what I've just done. I'm short of breath as panicky sobs start swelling up and popping in my chest and throat.

That was a bad idea. All of this. So bad.

My breath comes in jagged gasps as though it's harder to breathe than it is to cry, as if I'm actually drowning in my own tears.

I can't understand why I'm acting like this. It was sex. Just sex. No big deal.

But I'm lying because sex *is* a big deal – at least to me.

I squeeze my eyes shut and try not to think, but a blank mind is just a blank canvas for the images of what I've been doing to flash up; the dark ink of his new tattoo pressing against the white of my skin; the twist of his mouth; the moment when it went from something I wanted to be doing to something I wished would end. And when it did…

"Knew you'd be quality," he'd said, grinning at me like

we were the same, like I was the Ruby who flirted with him over beer and not the one hurriedly scrabbling for her clothes. Flirty Ruby would have laughed and told him he wasn't so bad himself.

That would have been a lie, just like the rest of it: the banter and the game-playing. "Quality" or not, I was only ever going to be another number and I wish with all my heart and soul that I hadn't been so *stupid* as to get caught up in it. For fuck's sake, that girl Kaya even said it…

"*Idiot,*" I hiss at myself, pressing my wrists into my eyes to rub away the tears. I automatically lift my index finger to wipe a smear of mascara from under my lash line, but when my hand comes up to my face I can smell him on my fingers and I'm reminded of the disgust I felt at how grubby he was.

What was I expecting? He'd just come offstage. When exactly would he have showered? Where?

Thank God for Kaz's mum and her embarrassingly large box of condoms. Thank God I took one, thank God I used it. I hope I put it on properly…

Please don't let me have caught anything… Please…

I start imagining that I've got gonorrhoea or chlamydia or worse and I want someone to come and tell me that I'm being silly and not to panic and that we'll go to the clinic and get me checked out and there's nothing to worry about because I didn't give him a blowjob despite the hints – "*It's not usually an issue*". For all I wanted to feel special at least one tiny sensible part of me must have known that I wasn't…

There is only one person I want right now.

Kaz.

But when I pull my phone out of my pocket and try to unlock the screen, I realize that I've left it too late. The battery is dead.

It's a long walk up to camp, but I can't think where else to go. The journey is exhausting and when I get there, all I find is the dead ash of last night's fire and four dark tents. Without much hope, I open ours and look inside.

Kaz isn't here. The only other place she might be is the Tom/Lauren camp, but even now, even though my pride is officially at an all-time low, I still have enough not to want Lauren to see me like this.

Shame clutches at my stomach, followed rapidly by an actual physical pang.

When did I last eat anything?

I dip into the pocket of my shorts, but all I've got is my dead phone, some change and the keys to Owen's van. Crawling back into the tent, I hunt for the packet of beef jerky I insisted we bring…

There's voices coming closer and I snap into full alert, hoping for Kaz or even Lee, but it's only Dongle and Parvati. She's giggling as he kisses her. "Stop mauling me!" she laughs, before pulling him back for another.

I clear my throat and Parvati pushes Dongle away so hard he nearly falls into the side of next door's tent.

"It's just me," I say, then, "You guys seen Kaz or Lee?"

There's an uncomfortable pause in which they look at

each other before shaking their heads in perfect time. Left, right, left, right, slow to centre.

"I'll leave you to it," I say and try for a kind of jock-like arm punch as I pass Dongle, but like everything about me, the gesture feels hollow and worthless. I head up the path towards Owen's van without looking back. I can't be here, in the tent, whilst Parvati's in Dongle's. Better to be alone in Owen's van with my beef jerky. And my misery.

The walk feels long. I'm weak and tired. There are a few people around, laughing, messing about by their tents and I find it hard to believe that away, in the distance, I can hear whoever's on the main stage. How is it not so much later? It's like time's folded in on itself and left me on the outside, looking in.

The car park looks different from yesterday – different in a way that's more than just light and dark – but once I get my bearings, Owen's van's not so hard to spot. All I want to do is open up one of the back doors, clamber in and shut out the world.

My eyes are half closed as I concentrate on turning the key in the lock. My whole body is ready to give up as I pull back the handle and swing the door open.

To find something that doesn't make sense. There's someone in the van—

No, two someones.

I don't—

"Fuck! Ruby!" It's Lee.

"Shit!" Not Lee. Not Owen. Not a boy I know.

My brain hasn't yet processed what I'm seeing, but my

body has decided that we're going to respond by running and I'm away from the van, darting between rows of cars, beyond the sight of my brother, who's shouting my name. I collapse against someone's car and press my face into my knees and try to think of something to block out what I've just seen.

My brain comes up with the faded photo that's up in the lounge – it's of all of us, taken when we were kids: seven-year-old Ed and four-year-old Callum, toddler Lee, and baby me, sitting on the floor in front. I'm zooming in on us, me squidged up and giggling in Lee's lap as he tickles me. It's like we don't even know someone's taking a photo; we're too busy hanging out. When I think about family and what it means to have one, I think about Lee's expression in that picture.

That look is my definition of love.

"Ruby?"

Lee is someone I have always trusted. He is a flake and a shit-stirrer. An infuriating piss-taker who can wind me up like no one else – not even Callum. But he is Lee. He's the person I wanted to be when I grew up.

I feel like I'm the one he's cheated.

"Ruby? Where are you?"

Lee's close by and I clench my teeth to stop myself from letting out the slightest sound as my shoulders shake.

"Please…"

He steps into view beyond my hiding place, his skinny white torso almost luminous in the moonlight. His shorts are still undone.

"Ruby." His voice is quiet enough that I wouldn't have heard him if I weren't so close. *"Please…"*

For a second I think I might call out, but then the other boy steps into view. I don't know him. I don't want to. I wish I could unknow his very existence. He puts a hand on Lee's shoulder and murmurs something.

"What?" Lee brushes him off. "Get a fucking clue. She's my sister, not my girlfriend."

The boy takes a step back and I catch sight of his features in the moonlight. He looks like all the boys Lee fancied before he met Owen. Wide-eyed and boyish. Slim. Lee doesn't even try to stop him as he walks away, just turns in the opposite direction.

I don't know how long I wait before I stand up and start walking. Long enough for my tears to have dried on my skin. Time's moved on and the campsite's heaving because the arena's tipped out and I walk, careless of where I'm actually going, until I wind to a halt near a hedge and step out of the lights marking the path until I'm deep in darkness, where no one will notice me. I slide onto the grass.

I can't talk to Kaz.

I can't talk to Lee.

And Owen…

I could never lie to him and I can't tell him the truth. Guilt and sadness sweep over me and I think how pathetic this makes me when Owen's the only one who has a right to this pain.

Dimly, I realize that someone's standing near by.

"You all right, pet?"

I shake my head and will him to leave.

He doesn't. "You shouldn't be here on your own. It's not safe."

Glancing up, I see that he's old. Mid-thirties. Skin pink from the sun, eyes pink from booze. Or weed.

"Not safe from people like you?" I say.

He shakes his head. "I'm not a crazy rapist. I've got chips." He holds a cone of chips towards me.

"Crazy rapists eat chips too."

The man shrugs and sits down a respectable distance from where I am. "Well, I'm not crazy and I'm not rapey. I'll just sit here. You sit there and I'll watch out for the rapists. OK?"

"Thanks," I say, and suddenly I'm pushed over the edge and I find myself sobbing into my hands, tears and snot squidging in the gaps between my fingers. He shuffles closer.

"I'm going to put an arm round you. Just shove me off if that's not OK."

But I don't. I lean in and I let this kind stranger hold me in a one-armed hug as I cry onto his shoulder, letting out everything that hurts until I'm just a Ruby-shaped shell of a human.

When he offers me a chip again, I take it. And then another until I find that I've eaten most of them.

It feels better to be full of chips than to be full of shame.

"You should find your friends." He folds the paper up

and asks if there's someone I'd like to call. I tell him my phone has died.

"Use mine." He hands it to me and waits. Of the three people whose numbers I know, it seems there's only one left I can call.

I'm beyond grateful when he answers and agrees to meet me at his camp. It isn't far from my hedge. The camp is dark and silent when I get there, right down to the figure standing by one of the tents. He doesn't move until I step into the circle.

"Ruby?" It is the voice Stu uses when there are no more games to be played.

"I have nowhere else to go." I'm shivering and he steps closer, but not close enough to hold me.

"What's wrong? Have you had a fight with Kaz or something?"

I nod. A fight with silence instead of words.

"Lee?"

My body does a violent judder at the mention of my brother and Stu steps forward then, his hands clamping round the tops of my arms to hold me steady. I wish he would pull me closer.

"You can't just ring me on a stranger's phone, tell me you need me and expect me to come running."

Even though I nod, I'm thinking that this is exactly what he has done. "I'm sorry. I'll go."

But when I twist away, he holds me fast.

"Why did you come here, then?" This time he's impatient. "Why did I leave Goz and Travis having fun on the other side of the campsite if you were just going to fuck off the second I arrived?"

"I don't know. You didn't have to."

Stu ducks his head until he's in my line of sight. "Look at me, Ruby. You called, I came. Enough of the bullshit. I know you – I know you so much better than you want me to. I know this isn't a game. I know something's really wrong. Just tell me."

I open my mouth to tell him, but I don't know where to start. With Kaz? With Adam Wexler? With Lee? And as all of the thoughts and feelings clamour to come out first, I say what it is that I really want.

"Can you just hug me? Please?"

Without a second's hesitation, Stu wraps his arms tight around my body and I'm sobbing into his chest as he kisses the top of my head and tells me that it's OK, everything will be all right, that he's sorry and he loves me and he's here for me.

Owen was right – you don't get to choose who loves you.

Here and now, when I most need holding, I believe that Stu means what he says.

SUNDAY

31 • HANDS OPEN

RUBY

My eyes feel gritty and my face is dry from the salt of too many tears. As I breathe in, the smell is one I have dreamed about too many times for it to feel true now. I stay where I am, wrapped in Stu's arms, his body curved round mine, spooning me. We're both clothed – although I had to take my vest off because it kept catching on everything. String vests are more hassle than they're worth.

When I open my eyes, the temptation to kiss his new tattoo is overwhelming, but I resist it the same way I resisted every fibre of wanting as I lay in his sleeping bag, his arms around me, and told him everything, about Kaz and Lauren, about Lee. Stu has always been easy to talk to – although I still couldn't tell him about the other thing. The further away it gets the more disgusted I feel about it. I just want to fold up the memory and hide it away, pretend it never happened.

I distract myself by kissing Stu's arm. Big mistake. Now I want to kiss all of him.

Stu mumbles something. He shuffles about in his sleep, making it easy for me to wriggle my way out of the sleeping bag. I can't be near him now I'm no longer asleep. At least when I'm unconscious, I'm incapable of acting on all the things I want to do.

I find his phone – he hasn't changed his pin since we split and I open up a new note.

Thank you for being there when I needed someone to hold me. Maybe me and you can be all right mates instead of trying to hurt each other? That would be happy-making.

I put the phone with the note open on the pillow next to his face, then I find my vest. My boots are outside... Time to go. Kissing my fingers, I press them lightly on his lips.

His eyes open as if he's been waiting for the right time to wake. Or the wrong time. Leaving him sleeping is easier than leaving him awake. I can't think what I'd have done without him last night, but today I need to find the strength to hold myself together – it feels too good to have Stu do it.

"Oh, you are so not just leaving me a note, Rubes."

"Um..."

Stu props himself up on one elbow and reads what I've written. "Come here."

"I've got to go."

"No, you don't." He's right in one way: I doubt Kaz is expecting me back at seven in the morning. And he's so very wrong in another: I've got to go because I can't be near him much longer.

"Please, just come here a second," he says. I shuffle back to the sleeping bag. "Closer, please." I get so close that my knees brush against his stomach. "Closer."

"I don't think—" But there's no arguing with the look

he's giving me and soon the only thing separating us is my refusal to give in to what I want the most.

"I need to tell you something, Ruby." When I look at him my heart aches. His eyes are darker than ever in the orange glow cast through the canvas and when he talks, his imperfect teeth are barely discernible from the tone of his skin. Stu should not be attractive: his nose is crooked beneath wild eyebrows and his skin's scarred from acne.

I could look at him for ever.

"It's all been a lie. The girls everyone's seen me with… You know none of it's true?"

"Even the one on my phone?" I mutter. "*Stella*. Girls have names, you know. They're not just walking vaginas."

But Stu's looking at me like he knows I'm trying to be difficult. "Stella was a spin-the-bottle kiss that I caught on camera because I was pissed at you for running off. You always do that. Push me away. You're doing it now." I swallow, I have nothing to say. I've been pushing him away from the second I pulled him. "There hasn't been anyone since you, Ruby. I'm fucking with your head because I can't fuck with your body." So romantic. "You're the only one I want to be with."

I shouldn't believe him. Stu is capable of saying he loves me whilst he's shaft-deep in someone else.

Isn't he?

"I can't do this, Stu. Not now."

"OK." He looks at me some more, then leans in and kisses me on the nose, tilting his forehead to rest on mine. "I know none of this changes what happened.

I'm sorry. It was the biggest mistake of my life."

The words stab into my guts. Guess I know more about making mistakes now than I did at the start of the summer. It's easier to sleep with the wrong person than I thought. And so much harder.

"I really do have to go," I say.

We stare at each other, drinking in everything about this time, when it is just him and me, and what we could have been if either of us were capable of having a relationship. If I hadn't spent all my time testing his limits – if his limits hadn't failed my tests.

Stu nods and stands, holding a hand to help me up. But as I rise, I see him watching me with sadness.

"Stu, I—"

He shakes his head and simply lifts my arm away from my body, reaching out with his other hand to brush the backs of his fingers softly, slowly, sadly down my ribcage.

"If I can't take care of you, please will you take care of yourself?"

And I nod before stepping away and looking at Stu one last time as if he's the thing I need to nourish me.

KAZ

For the first time since we arrived, I take something out of our food store. The excitement with which I planned our meals seems like a lifetime ago. The beans we'd bought, Ruby sneaking ones with hot dogs into the basket when she thought I wasn't looking, remain untouched. Just like the beef jerky that Ruby insisted "goes with everything" and has been eaten with nothing. Although when I look for it, I realize that's gone, like the person who bought it.

All I have to go on is a message she sent me late last night: *Staying with a friend. R*

As if I no longer qualify. I'm assuming that friend must be Stu, since that's the number from which the message was sent. I called back, but no one answered. Just as I'm free from Tom, Ruby's lost to Stu. The irony is painful.

Tipping my cornflakes into what I think is a camping bowl, I go through ten tiny cartons of UHT that Ruby stole from the coffee station at The Rock Shop before I get bored and eat the cereal mostly dry, sitting in the doorway of the tent, my toes in the cool grass. Above, the sky is lank and grey, suffocating us with stillness. The bunting that Owen put up is now flattened on the floor next to something that I pray is a dropped curry, but is more likely to be an unsavoury substance hurled from the pit of someone's stomach.

Someone unzips the tent opposite and Owen emerges. There's no sign of Lee in the tent behind him.

"I'm going to get a coffee. Want anything?" he asks.

"A coffee as big as you can buy it. Milk no sugar."

"No sign of Ruby?"

I shake my head. Last night I texted him that I'd had a message from her and he'd replied saying that Dongle and Parvati had seen her and she'd looked tired but fine.

I swallow a particularly sharp mouthful of cornflakes. "What about Lee?"

"You can ask him yourself when he wakes up." Owen

points at the girls' tent and there's a pause in which I acknowledge that this is not the time to ask. "Turned up looking for Ruby not long after you went to bed. I passed on the message."

This strikes me as odd. When Ruby can't find me, she has always turned to Lee.

What happened last night?

Owen's left when there's a curse as someone narrowly avoids stepping in the curry (vomit) and stumbles into the middle of our camp.

RUBY

"Hi," I say when Kaz looks up.

"Hi" is all I get in reply. She's eating cornflakes with a chip fork out of a pan meant for boiling on the stove.

"How are the cornflakes?" It's the only thing that springs to mind.

"Cornflakey. Would you like some?"

I wouldn't, but I suppose I've got to eat something and cereal seems like an easy place to start. Kaz sets about prepping a bowl/pan for me and I help by opening the milk and tipping it in. I seriously underestimated how much to bring. Or accurately estimated since we've not needed any milk until now.

"I'm sorry about last night," I say, letting the cereal soften slightly in the hopes I'll find it easier to eat.

"Me too," Kaz says. "Lauren had a panic attack in the crowd and we had to take her to the first-aid tent."

"Oh." That is not what I thought had happened. "Why didn't you say?"

"I did. Text. Call. You didn't answer, Ruby."

"Sorry. Battery died." And I was so caught up in the excitement of Wexler that I didn't even think to check. So sure that Kaz had simply wanted to be with Lauren more than me that I didn't think I needed to. "Is Lauren OK?"

"I think so." Kaz stabs her cornflakes a little viciously. "Tom's with her now, so…" She shrugs.

"Babysitting duties are over."

"Something like that."

Kaz looks at me, making me uncomfortably aware that I'm still poking at my cereal instead of eating it. I draw lines across the bowl, mentally dividing it into four manageable chunks and start on the first.

"Ruby. What happened?"

Hands running over bodies. Teeth on skin. Sobs that sounded like pleasure. The smell of sweat and alcohol and something chemical that I can't quite place.

I feel dirty and used and stupid.

"You look really upset. What did he do?"

I glance up sharply. *How does she know?*

"If Stu hurt you…"

I'm confused. "Stu hasn't done anything."

"You don't have to lie to me, Ruby."

I give up on my breakfast and put it down with relief. Holding it was tiring.

"Look." Kaz shuffles close enough that I can smell her deodorant, reminding me that I've got to get clean.

"I know I've not been here for you the last couple of days, and I'm so sorry, but I'm here now."

KAZ

Ruby isn't speaking. Even breathing seems hard and she's drawing in air like she's about to be sick, but I am not making yesterday's mistakes today.

When Ruby says nothing, it's because she doesn't know how to ask for help – and if she's about to be sick, she'll have to hurl on my shoulder.

I reach in for a hug and Ruby flings her arms around me, clinging tight.

RUBY

I don't care that Kaz is offering this hug for all the wrong reasons, to comfort me for something she thinks happened with Stu when it happened with someone else. Someone I don't think I will ever be able to admit to. I no longer want Kaz to make it real. I just want her to make it go away.

KAZ

There's a tremor in her chest and I realize that Ruby's crying.

How do I handle this? Ruby *never* cries. She's the one who teases me for crying all the time – at *Hollyoaks*, old people holding hands on the seafront, lost-pet posters, war poetry, Naomi deliberately bending the nib of my favourite fountain pen, John Lewis Christmas adverts – the only time she ever cried at school was when she tripped running down to the hockey pitch and slid across the gravel on bare legs, her momentum broken when her face came into contact with Kirsten Turner's left boot.

"I'm so sorry I wasn't there for you, Ruby. No one should be able to do this to you. You're worth so much more than this."

As I say the words they sound like an echo of what my sister said. *Even you can do better*. I hope Ruby pays more attention to what I'm saying than I did to Naomi.

32 • IT'S GOING TO TAKE SOME TIME

KAZ

Ruby insists she needs a shower, which sounds like a nice idea until I discover that the ones on-site are communal.

"You can take a leopard to a festival, but you can't make it wash its spots off in public," she teases me and I don't mind one bit because it's the first time I've seen her smile since yesterday. "Any chance you could top my phone up at the charging tent?"

She hands me her phone and glances at mine, which has been buzzing all the way here. I'm well aware who it is. So's Ruby.

"You should go and see him," she says so quietly that I'm convinced I've misheard. "I've been a dick about you and Tom and Lauren and … everything."

"You haven't." But we both know she has.

"You don't get to choose how you feel about someone, right?"

I worry anew about what happened with Stu, but there's time enough for that later. "I should go and see Tom. Sort things out."

"What kind of things?"

"I'll tell you later." I give her a hug. "Promise."

Tom's left a voicemail: *Meet me down by the coffee stalls at the bottom of the hill — wherever you are, you can't be far away. We need to talk sooner rather than later. Before ... well, before we see each other in the arena."*

I'm confused, but then I notice the message I've got from Lauren.

Thank you so much for taking care of me yesterday! Can't wait to see you later and get the gossip on Sebastian! xxx

I wonder whether she's told Tom? Not that it's any of his business.

After dropping Ruby's phone off at the charging tent, I go and meet him.

He's sitting at one of the picnic tables set up by the largest cluster of food vans. For a second, I pause and look at him. Tom has been the person I've wanted for so long that it's hard to see what he really looks like sometimes. In my mind, everything I like about him is enhanced, the bits I'm not so convinced of glossed over and forgotten: the trousers that Naomi and Ruby find so hilarious that show half-an-inch too much of his socks; the way one corner of his permanently popped collar always wilts over; his habit of biting his cuticles until they bleed. He's doing it now and at the sight of it my nose wrinkles.

I think of Sebastian's calloused fingers, strong and slender, and the ease with which he slid them between mine.

When Tom turns this way the automatic assumption that I love him no longer feels true.

"I got you a coffee," he says when he sees me.

I take a sip and nearly dribble it back into the cup. "Is there sugar in this?" He nods and I frown. "When have I ever taken—"

Both of us realize at the same time that this is how Lauren takes her coffee and I carry it to the nearest bin and drop it in, not caring one little bit that Tom will hate to see it wasted.

We walk along the path until we're in the quiet of the woods, where the air is heavier and more stifling and we sit, side by side, on a fallen log. There's room for another person between us, even if she isn't here.

Tom starts. "Thank you for yesterday."

I wait, but he doesn't appear to have anything more to say.

"Is that it?" I say, for once sounding as outraged as I feel.

Tom is unprepared for this — it's nothing like the Kaz I've been so far. "I've said thanks. What more do you want?"

"Are you for real, Thomas?" I sound like his mum. Or my sister. "How about an apology?"

"For what?"

"For *everything*? For lying to me, for having sex with me, for having the nerve yesterday to ask me to look after your new girlfriend?"

"You could have said no."

"You could have told me you had a girlfriend!" Our voices are getting louder with every retort.

"You could have asked!"

"Why would I need to? You're *Tom*. Don't you understand? You're the boy I've been half in love with since I was ten. I'm not supposed to need to ask that Tom the truth. He's supposed to tell me."

"I did." His voice has dropped and he has the good

grace to look uncomfortable.

"Too late." That's it. My anger has burned itself out. "Everything. All of it. It's too late."

He'd asked for the weekend to make it right and told me that I'm the one he wants, but there is nothing that can make this right and I do not want him. Not any more.

"So what now?" He's looking at his hands; his cuticles are ragged and sore-looking, as if he's done nothing but bite them for the last twenty-four hours.

"I don't know, Tom."

"So you don't want me to break up with her?"

"I don't want anything from you."

"Not even to be friends?"

"Not right now, no." Only when he looks at me, I don't see my ex-boyfriend. I see the boy whose house I lived in the summer my parents got divorced, who made room for me, made time for me, who heard me singing in the spare bedroom and told me I sounded like Karen Carpenter because he knew it would cheer me up. "But I'm sure we can find our way back there. Eventually."

There's a long silence in which I strain to hear the sounds of the campsite and Tom sips from what must now be a cold cup of tea.

"I'm sorry, Kaz," he says.

It's been a long time coming, but those words make all the difference and when he looks at me, I give him what must be an encouraging smile, because he reaches over and hugs me. The feel of him, the smell, no longer thrills me. It just makes me sad.

I'm the first to let go.

"What about Lauren?" I ask.

Tom looks shifty and I know now what I should have known from the start: he is not going to break up with her.

"You're not going to tell her, are you?" I say.

But Tom doesn't quite answer. "Are you?"

Not so long ago, I believed that the truth was enough to make things right, but it's hard to see how it will now.

"I don't want Lauren to know what happened." I feel terrible for saying it.

"Me neither."

"If you cheat on her again…" I say, but what threat am I really making?

"I would *never*." Tom is vehement, but then, he would have been before. "I really do like her. She doesn't deserve any of this."

"Lauren deserves a lot better." The way he avoids looking at me, Tom knows I mean better than him. Soon we'll make our way back to our camps and when I see him later (and I will, because how can I avoid the pair of them in the arena without it looking suspicious?), I don't want this to have been our goodbye. We need to behave like friends, not like a mistake.

When we stand to leave, I bump him gently and smile, trying to make it right, to make it light. "I'm not sure it matters, but your new girlfriend has my seal of approval."

"It matters," he says, and for a second he looks at me like he wishes it didn't. "Bye, Kaz."

He walks quickly towards the path leading across

Three-Tree Field and I want to call him back, to ask him the one question that's been plaguing me, burrowing into my brain.

Did you sleep with her before you slept with me?

But I don't. It's hard to see how the truth will make that right either.

33 • BITTERSWEET ME

RUBY

It's oddly peaceful here in the tent and I feel better for having had a shower. On the way back to the tent, my gut twisted when I passed a girl wearing a Gold'ntone T-shirt. The realization that I will never be able to listen to their music again rips me a new one. I will *never* be able to hear "Tonight Too Soon" ever again.

I shouldn't have let Kaz believe this was Stu's fault, but I cannot tell her – *anyone* – the truth. Memories fade with time, but words spoken out loud become facts.

I can't face these facts. Not now. Not ever.

"Ruby. Can I come in?" It's Lee, outside the tent.

I don't say anything.

"I know you're in there. Please, Ruby."

I crawl out of the tent, wrapping my arms around myself, rumpling the whimsical unicorn vest that I bought when I felt distinctly more whimsical.

"What?" I can barely look at him.

"Not here…" He casts a glance to where Owen and Anna are cooking breakfast.

When Lee turns to walk away, I follow. His neck is sunburned and I imagine flicking it hard enough to make him howl. When we reach the path, Lee keeps pausing to let me fall in step with him, but since that is what I'm specifically avoiding doing, I fall out as soon as he starts up again.

It is very satisfying.

Eventually, we reach a quiet patch of the campsite where the tents thin out towards the car park and Lee sits down.

"Are you going to sit with me, or stay standing there like Christ the Redeemer?" he says.

"Why do you do that?" I snap, wanting a fight.

"What?"

"Make a reference to something you know I won't understand. You used to hate it when Callum did that and now you're doing it to me. Showing off doesn't make you special."

"I'm not showing off. This is just how I talk."

"Frankly, Mr Shankly, you sound a bit wanky." But he's not going to take the bait.

"I know that's some music reference you think I won't get." Lee sighs and lies back on the ground. "Call it even and sit down."

I do as I'm told.

Lee says, "You didn't tell Owen." Not a question, so I don't give an answer. "Thank you for that."

This galls. "As if I'd inflict that kind of pain on someone I love so much."

"Stop being so angry with me. Not everything you see is black and white, you know."

"Was the man in the van Owen? No. Enough said."

"Actually" – Lee sits up and pulls my arm so I'm

twisted to face him – "not enough said. Owen and I broke up. On Friday."

"*Friday?*"

"After I behaved like a dick about him singing—"

"But I thought…" I'd seen them hugging outside their tent, but then every time I've seen them together since then, at camp, on the hill, the photo he texted of them in the crowd … I realize I saw no kisses. No hand-holding. No glances or touches. I carried on seeing what I wanted to, even when it wasn't there. That hug I saw was one of breaking-up, not making-up.

"We thought it would make things awkward for everyone else and that wouldn't be fair," Lee says quietly, pulling tufts of shrivelled grass from the ground.

"But you *love* him."

Lee looks at me with such misery that I can't help but soften towards him. "You think I was the one who did it? I'm not the strong one. I'm the coward who'd rather spend a summer spoiling for a fight than face telling the person I love the truth."

"But *Owen* loves you—"

"Love isn't enough, Ruby. Not to survive me moving half a world away. I can't be the boyfriend Owen deserves and he knows it."

His eyes shine with unshed tears, the deep blue that circles the skies of his irises more marked, as if his eyes were drawn, then filled in.

"I don't want to leave him." Tears spill out and he sniffs. "But I can't take him with me and I can't do long distance

and all that would happen is that I'd hurt him even more."
Lee's crying properly now, shaking as he talks, the words
sputtering on breaths he can't quite take in.

"I love him so much, but I'm so weak that I can't even
do my own dirty work. He told me that if it would stop me
from trying to hurt him, then we should end things now,
because ..."

He stops and sucks in a breath, and I can't help but
reach over and wipe away his tears. I wish I could help fix
him, but it's him that's doing the breaking.

"... because he still wants to love me, even if we're not
together. Even if we can't be ... because I..." Lee breaks
down and I hold him as close as I can. "Why did I do this,
Ruby? What's wrong with me that I have to push away the
one person I want to be with?"

I hold him, saying nothing because there is nothing I
can say.

Maybe I did grow up to be like my brother after all.

KAZ

In the haze of euphoria that comes with finally doing
something right, I do something completely out of character.

"Why are you ringing me?" my sister asks when she picks
up the call.

"Hi, Naomi, how lovely to hear your voice."

"It's ten in the morning. Your voice is ruining my lie-in."

"I thought you'd be halfway down Oxford Street by now."

"Sunday. Shops don't open till later. Plus Dad's demanded

a break, the lame ass. How's your crappy festival?"

"You don't really care, do you?"

"Not at all, but I'm weirded out by you ringing me. It's making me come over all polite."

Which is her way of showing concern, I suppose. "You were right."

"Always. Be more specific."

"About Tom. About me deserving better."

"That doesn't sound like something I'd say…"

But we both know she did.

"Whatever we had, it's over now. I don't want him back any more." Saying it sets me free.

"You don't *sound* like you're a pathetic, weeping, wailing blob of snot…"

"Charming." I laugh. "That's because I know it's the right thing this time."

"It was the right thing last time."

"All right, no need to be smart about it. I just wanted to tell" – I was going to say "someone", but – "you."

Silence. My sister doesn't really know how to handle me being nice to her. I wouldn't either, if the situation was reversed.

"So now I've woken you up, can you do me a favour?" My tone makes it clear the conversation is back to normal.

So is Naomi's. "Probably not."

"Ring Mum. Ask her about her date last night – it's not just me she wants to gossip with."

As I end the call, I'm level with the charging tent and I collect Ruby's phone, before turning back towards our camp. My thoughts drift to Sebastian and I smile at the thought of telling Ruby about all the good things that have happened this weekend, as well as the bad. Because I'm going to tell her everything now – as Ruby said, she and I don't do secrets.

I'm distracted as Ruby's phone starts to vibrate and a message flashes up.

Hey, Ruby, on the off chance you've charged your phone… I'm at your camp. Where are you? Stu

34 • CARELESS WHISPER

RUBY

After a while Lee asks me how he looks.

"Puffy" is my answer.

"But in a cute way, right?"

"If you find blotches and snot cute, then sure, why not?"

He hauls me up off the floor and we walk back side by side. I don't know what my brother is thinking about, but for the most part I'm thinking that Lee has only partially explained what happened last night and for all I want to be able to leave it as it is, I can't.

"Lee?"

"Yes?"

"Why did you do it?"

He doesn't ask what I mean – he knows I mean the boy he was with, the not-Owen whose shorts Lee had been unzipping. "I told you, Ruby, I'm weak. And I thought it would make me feel better to know I could be with someone I didn't love."

The thought process is so alarmingly familiar that it knocks the breath out of me.

I don't want Wexler to be Stu – that's kind of the point.

But it didn't make me feel better, and looking at Lee, I'm not sure it worked out for him either.

"But in *Owen's van*? What were you thinking?"

Lee shrugs. "I have spare keys. Thought it'd be better than bringing him back to Owen's tent."

I give him Ultimate Disapproval Face.

And then, as if it has only just occurred to him, his brows pull together and he tilts his face to look at me closely.

"What were *you* doing there?"

KAZ

Camp is deserted but for a lone figure standing, hands in pockets, waiting for someone who isn't me.

"What are you doing here?" I say.

Stu turns at the sound of my voice. He looks exhausted and he hasn't shaved since Friday – although the way he smells I guess he's washed. Stu always smells good. Pheromones from his sex overdrive, presumably.

"I'm looking for Ruby. Do you know where she is?"

"Why, so you can just keep hurting her?"

Stu looks confused. "What do you mean?"

"That I don't want you anywhere near her."

"Seriously, we're still doing that? You telling me what Ruby wants when you're the one who hurts her the most?"

"*Me?*" I can't even believe he's saying it. "You *cheated* on her."

"Oh, for fuck's sake!" Stu snaps his head back and stares at the sky, before glaring at me. "Will you let it go?

"How can I? You CHEATED on her!" How loud do I

have to say it for him to hear?

"I made a mistake. One that *you*" – he points not just with his finger, but his eyes, his voice, his whole being – "won't let me forget."

"Because you were going to carry on as if nothing happened!"

Like Tom is doing with Lauren. But Stu is not Tom. Stu would have done it again…

"What if I *had* carried on as if nothing happened? What. Fucking. If? Did you ever, for a second, allow for the tiniest possibility that I made her happy? That for all you think I'm a toxic landfill of a human being, I didn't love her?"

"You'd a funny way of showing it," I say quietly.

"You think being in love is the same as being perfect, do you?" For the first time I see something more than a caricature of a slutty sex god, I see someone who feels pain and hope. And regret. "Do you really believe that love makes you a better person?" *God knows it has made me worse.* "Well, it doesn't work like that. It makes me want to try, but that's the best I can do – and you won't even let me have that."

But he hasn't been here to see the mess he's made of my friend this weekend, the shell of the Ruby *I* love who walked into camp this morning.

"The only way you know how to try is to hurt her, Stu." My voice is quiet, but clear. He does not need to take a step closer to hear it, but he does anyway.

"You think I did so much damage when I slept with another girl, but even Ruby knows my heart wasn't in it.

You talk about cheating like it's the worst thing that could happen. But you and Lauren? That's betrayal on a level I couldn't hope to achieve…"

"Don't say that." I don't want to hear this. Not at all. "It's not true."

"You mean more to Ruby than I ever could. Where were you last night, Kaz, when Ruby needed you? With Lauren? And *why*? Just because you feel so guilty that you've been fucking Lauren's boyfriend?"

Stu's almost shouting, but my voice comes out as a horrified whisper. "What? I didn't…"

"Come off it!" Stu laughs at me, a short sharp bark. "You can fool Ruby. You can fool Lauren. But you can't fool the guy who saw you leave Tom's tent, your bra in your hand and tears down your face." Ice-cold dread floods through me as I picture bumping into Stella. I'd been so keen on running away I hadn't taken the time to notice who she was with. "Because you found out that Saint Thomas of Selkirk's as much of a dog as me. That he'd do you the same time he's banging someone else."

"I didn't know about Lauren," I whisper, not sure who I'm trying to convince.

"You didn't want to." Stu looks at me like he's always had the truth of it. "Tell me, Kaz, are you going to do for your new BFF what you did for your old one? You going to give Tom the same ultimatum you gave me?" It's as if he's shining a light into the deepest darkest places where the guilt, the hypocrisy is cosseted in the bubble wrap of self-righteousness. But Stu isn't finished unpacking me.

"Guess it's harder this time. Tom didn't cheat with some stranger, a girl she'll never have to meet, a girl who *meant nothing* – you're going to have to tell Lauren that her boyfriend had sex with *you*."

In that one, two, heartbeats, there is no sound, there is nothing outside of my world except those words.

And then…

A half-sob.

Life is happening in slow motion. I turn so slowly that she's already turned to run from what she's heard.

Not Ruby: Lauren.

RUBY

Lee and I are nearly back at camp. He knows I lied when I said I went to Owen's van because I needed some space away from Kaz and Lauren, but he didn't push it.

"Speak of the devil." Lee points at someone running through the tents, stumbling over the guy ropes. The sound of her sobs reaches us, and we glance at each other, confused. I'm about to tell him to go after her, when we see Kaz hurrying down the path towards us. "Sorry, excuse me please… Oh, just… OUT OF THE WAY!" she shouts at a group of boys who are having a piggy-back fight.

"Kaz!" I catch her arm. "What's going on? Is everything OK?"

"I'm so sorry, Ruby. I've got to find Lauren." She looks frantic and I let go of her arm. Lee points in the direction Lauren went and Kaz rushes on a few steps before spinning back. "Your phone, take it, take it…"

I take it.

"I'll call you as soon as I've fixed things. I'll meet you in the arena." She closes the distance between us and gives me a hug. "I'm sorry. Stu's looking for you. Don't let him get to you."

"OK…" I pat her back, wondering why I'm getting such a desperate hug.

"I love you, Ruby."

"Um…"

"You know that, right?" She pulls back from the hug to look at me so intently it's quite scary.

"Kaz, are you *dying*?"

"No. Just making a mess of absolutely everything." And then she's off again.

KAZ

Where's she gone? The crowd is so much larger today and I despair of finding her. I feel like such a bad human being on so many levels that I almost give up there and then. Until…

There. And even though I'd rather be running in the other direction I plunge forward.

Lauren's stalled by the crowds at the gate, but the queue is knotted too tightly for me to get through. I call Tom.

"Lauren knows!" I say by way of greeting.

"She—" There's a beep on his phone and a pause as he checks the message. "Oh. I just got a text…" – which I assume he's reading – "What the *hell*, Kaz? I thought we agreed—"

"*I* didn't tell her!" I'm angry. "She heard Stu shout that you slept with me when you were supposed to be sleeping with her."

There's a (presumably) stunned silence on the other end of the phone, during which time I manage to process the meaning behind what I've just said, the question I hadn't meant to ask – the answer Tom is not giving.

It's the last, undeniable piece of the puzzle: the condoms in his bag; the girlfriend sharing his tent; the way Lauren talked… And yet I talked myself out of all of those things because I still wanted to believe in a Tom that didn't exist.

I'm *so* stupid.

"… are you now?" Oh. Tom is talking.

And I'm angry.

"In the arena. I'm going to find Lauren," I say.

No, *furious*.

"KAZ, DON'T—"

Make that apoplectic.

"Sod off, Tom. It's not like you're capable of making it better, either." And I hang up for good.

I'm never answering one of his calls again.

RUBY

Stu is at our camp. I honestly have no idea what has gone down, but he does not look happy.

God, I love him.

No, that's not right.

Lee's ahead of me, barging towards my ex-boyfriend. "What are you doing here?"

"What do you think I'm doing here? Looking for Ruby." Stu tries to look round my brother, but Lee leans to block his view.

"Well, she's not here."

"She's *right there*, you twat, I can see her with my eyes."

"What are you doing, Lee?" I elbow him out of the way. "Hello, Stu."

He reaches out to touch my arm, but Lee bats his hand away.

"Get off my sister!"

"What?!" I'm not sure who's more outraged, me or Stu.

"I'm looking out for you, Ruby."

"For fuck's—" Stu makes a frustrated growling noise in his throat. "What's with the 'Must Protect Ruby' mandate? First Kaz, now you."

"What happened with Kaz?" I ask, trying to change the subject.

Stu actually looks a little guilty. "I don't want to fuck it up any further than I already have. This is something you need to talk to Kaz about."

Which is all very mysterious. And annoying. I don't like people not telling me things.

HYPOCRITE KLAXON!

"Stop changing the subject." Lee is talking. "You've been screwing with Ruby all weekend."

"And you're going to stop me." Stu rolls his eyes. "Seriously, Lee. I mean, *seriously.*" He steps a little closer, crossing his arms to make his biceps look bigger. Next to my brother he doesn't really need to. I've got bigger biceps than him and I look like a starved chicken. Well, a mutant chicken who has biceps.

"You dare lay another finger on her..." Lee is actually squaring up to him and I can't help it.

Laughter explodes from me so hard that I feel like all the misery, all the regret, all the energy from the crowds, the music, *everything* is spilling out of me. I'm bending over double, my stomach killing me, and I'm aware that my brother and the boy I'm not supposed to love are staring at me like I've lost my mind.

Maybe I kinda have.

KAZ

It seems as if the sun is sitting on top of the clouds as they bulge lower under the weight of it, pressing down on the air. Sweat prickles lightly on my top lip as I step out into the arena, despairing at the crowds in here, doubting that I'll find her. I've tried ringing, but she's turned her phone off.

Poor Lauren. I don't know how I would react if I were in her position.

Tom didn't cheat with some stranger, a girl she'll never have to meet, a girl who meant nothing – *you're going to have to tell Lauren that her boyfriend had sex with you.*

I don't want to apologize to Lauren (well, I do, but I know it will mean almost nothing). I don't even know what I want to say to her. I just know I have to find her.

I'm wandering aimlessly through the crowds when I catch sight of a red vest in the crowd ahead. Slowly, I walk down from the brow of the hill to where Lauren is sitting, alone on the grass.

She's been crying. Who wouldn't have?

"Hello, Kaz." She doesn't sound angry. Nor does she look up.

I sit, knees pulled up to my chin, skirt over my legs so that I can just feel the hem brushing my bare toes. There's a long, depressing silence, as if I can't read the score I'm supposed to be playing from. Best improvise.

"I'm sorry you found out like that."

"I'm sorry there was something for me to find out about," she says, still not looking at me.

"I'm so sorry…"

But Lauren isn't listening. "I knew this was coming. I just thought I could stop it. If you and I became friends… I didn't know it was already too late."

I close my eyes against the bright grey of the sky and think how *furious* I am with Tom. If I had met Lauren – if I'd even known she existed – all this could have been prevented. "I didn't know he was seeing someone else."

Lauren shakes her head and laughs without mirth. "Neither did his parents until Tom invited me round for one of their barbecues. You should have seen the look on their faces… And all the relatives asked where you were, not by your title, but by your name. *Where's Kaz? Aren't the two of you still friendly? Such a lovely girl.* I don't think they were trying to be rude or anything. They just missed you. And then, I think, Tom did too. I'd catch him looking at photos on his phone or listening to Carpenters songs on repeat."

This makes me incredibly sad. That's exactly what I had been doing.

"But Tom's the kind of boyfriend I've always wanted.

Apart from the being in love with his ex-girlfriend thing. I thought I could change his mind. Show him what we had was something worth having." She finally looks at me and my whole body becomes an echo chamber of guilt. "Guess I wasn't worth that much to him after all."

It's so difficult to look at her when I say, "If I'd known…"

"Did you ask him?" And I move my head ever so slightly from side to side. "Perhaps you should have done."

When Lauren looks away, I'm relieved. Eye contact is hard. A tear drips from her cheek onto her vest, blooming a deeper red as if she's been cut.

"I feel like such a fool," she says.

"You're not. You haven't been." I'm on the verge of tears too, even though I don't deserve to be sad. "I'm so sorry. God. I can't say it enough."

Lauren laughs, a tired, humourless "Huh!" then, "No. You really can't."

And when she looks at me, I force myself to face the consequences of what I've done. "I really like you, Lauren." Because there is nothing else left to say.

"I really liked you too."

We sit there for a moment, both looking anywhere but at each other, neither sure what comes next, when I feel Lauren tense beside me.

"Kaz…" One hand is rising up to her mouth in surprise, but the other is pointing at the Festblog screen. "Is that *Ruby*?"

36 • ALL EYES ON ME

RUBY

Stu is currently timing how fast I can eat a hot dog. Lee walked with us to the arena, but left us to go and find the others. I'm quite glad, since having him shoot Stu evils every other second might have put me off my hot-dog-gobbling game. As it is, I am totally nailing this. It's like a snake swallowing an egg. My cheeks are stuffed, so I punch Stu on the arm to indicate he needs to stop the clock, but he shakes his head.

"Oh no, you've got to swallow it."

I almost choke on the last swallow before I come back with, "You would say that…"

And he gives me a wicked grin, his teeth flashing a touch, before he looks down at the clock on his phone. "Well done. Record time, Soho."

I love it when he calls me that. My favourite of the Ruby song references.

"So what do I win?" I look up at him, meeting his eyes, trying not to smile too wide.

"Did I say there was a prize?" But he's watching me for something. Something I want him to see. Stu edges closer, his lower lip tucked into his mouth thoughtfully, piercing bobbing as he plays with it. When he's close enough, Stu slides his arms around me and presses his lips to mine and I let it happen. I have always resisted the idea of giving Stu what he wants, even when we were together. But I'm thinking that maybe it's OK to give someone what they want, if that's what you want too.

And it is what I want. *He* is what I want, flaws and all. When he gets it right, Stu makes me happy like no one else. Besides, he's not the only one who's flawed, is he?

When Stu pulls away, he is smiling with every fibre of his being and I feel like I am the only person in his world.

"Is that her?" Whoever says this is speaking so loud that I look up, wondering who she's pointing at.

It's me.

Her friends shake their heads, and try to turn her away, one of them smiling an apology as they pass. But I can hear the girl muttering, "I'm sure it's her. Look at that tattoo on her arm."

Stu and I glance down at my arm and I shrug. "Someone's a fan of my fake tatt."

Stu checks the time and asks me if I'd like to head down to the main stage. The next band coming on are a hardcore act that have had a few top 40 hits – the words "pit" and "epic" are thrown in, not that I need convincing. But as we walk down to the main stage, I start to feel paranoid. It really does seem like people are looking at me. Stu notices too, because when someone shouts "Get in!" he gives me a worried look and slides his hand into mine.

We crest the hill and start walking down towards the stage. I glance up at the Festblog screen when it starts flashing red.

The banner across the top of the screen says:

GOSSIP SO HOT WE'RE BURNING YOU TWICE!!!

Seriously. Who writes this crap?

And then:

Adam Wexler – or should that be SEXler?

Just the sight of his name is enough to close my throat so tight I can't even draw breath.

But then there's a picture of him. A fuzzy snap taken on a camera phone as he's sitting at a table in the sunshine with a girl. Kissing.

My lungs tourniquet as I see myself on screen.

There's an arrow pointing at on-screen me.

WHO'S THIS CUTIE?!

And then there's a shot of Wexler walking with me towards the Gold'ntone bus…

There's another helpful arrow.

GOLD'NTONE'S TOUR BUS…

Oh God.

This time there's a shot of me, falling out of the bus, my clothes dishevelled, hair all over the place, my bra strap slipped halfway down the arm with the ink. Then some text flashes up.

SEXY WEXY KNOWN FOR HIS FAN-FANCYING SCORES A HOTTIE.

BUT WHO IS SHE?

The tension that's twisted my respiratory system into a halt snaps and suddenly I'm breathing fast and shallow. *Why are they doing this?*

"Ruby – what…?" Stu reaches for me, but I push him

out of the way so I can see the screen.

There I am. The stupid fucking photo that those girls took of me backstage.

"Is that *you?*" some boy near by asks.

"You. Fuck off." Stu turns to point at whoever's talking.

"All right, mate. Not my fault your bird's screwing around—" Stu steps towards him, away from me, and that's my chance.

I run. Again. Always fucking running.

KAZ

I try ringing her. Again and again and again, but it rings out each time.

Then I ring Lee, who isn't answering either, and I leave a slightly garbled message, the gist of which is, "Where is Ruby?"

I call my mum by accident and hang up and hope she won't notice the missed call.

I call Owen, who does answer, and I have to shout at him because of the noise in the background, until I give up and text him. My hands are shaking too much and Lauren takes the phone off me: *Meet at the spot on the hill. Check Festblog – explains the emergency.*

Ruby will be hating this, people knowing her business...

Why didn't she tell me *her business?* But a nasty little voice that sounds a lot like Stuart Garside pipes up, *Where were you last night when she needed you?*

My breaths don't seem to be coming in properly and I need a second to calm down, asking Lauren to call Stu.

I can't believe that I'm actually hoping she's with him.

"Stu? It's Lauren on Kaz's—" Lauren frowns. "Where is she now?"

RUBY

I'm about to be sick as I catapult into the toilets. The nice ones down by the front of the stage that are a bit Porta-kabin-y. Only they're not so nice after a day and a half's use. The cubicle I cannoned into is coated in diarrhoea and I back out quickly. Not there.

"Yeah. You know there's a queue, yeah?"

I hadn't even registered the fact there was a queue.

"Sorry," I say quietly. "Thought I was going to be sick."

The feeling has gone – presumably put off by the sight of what I was planning on being sick into.

"Yeah, sorry. But if you're not, yeah, there's still a queue."

I nod meekly and join the back of the four-person line. We shuffle forwards until I'm level with the sinks, where I study my arm in the mirrors. The girl who's washing her hands tells me my tattoo looks pretty. I think about the picture on the screens, how prominent my arm is in every single one of the shots with Wexler.

I've got to get it off.

KAZ

Once we've all gathered together – Stu too – I take charge, sending Lee up to the Festblog tent to see if we can stop them posting it again – she's *sixteen*, this can't be legal. Owen is going back to our camp in case Ruby's hiding there, and Anna and Dongle say they'll check the stalls. I ask Lauren and Parvati to check the two different girls' loos at the top of the hill. I'll go for the ones by the main stage.

When I turn to face Stu, I feel like crying. If I hadn't been so intent on blaming this on him, maybe Ruby would have had a chance to tell me the truth. Two days ago I wouldn't have believed it possible that Ruby Kalinski would not ring me *immediately* if she so much as spoke to Adam Wexler, let alone *slept* with him. How did we get like this?

"Why are you crying?" Stu looks at me fiercely. "Don't fucking fall apart now. This isn't about you or Lauren or Lee or me. It's about Ruby."

"I thought it was you – I'm sorry," I say, but he shakes his head.

"Yeah, well, you made a mistake." And he turns up the hill to check the line of tents up there.

I suppose we all make mistakes – it's how we deal with them that matters.

Maybe my biggest mistake was that I never let Stu deal with his in the first place.

37 • KISS WITH A FIST

RUBY

The toilets have become less crowded as I stand, raking the flesh on my left arm, scrubbing and sobbing as the stains on my skin remain. My skin's red from the effort and my hand's numb from the cold, cold water.

"Come on." My voice is feeble, falling out of my mouth between dry sobs. "Just … come … off…"

I give up for a second, folding my arms across the sink and resting my head on them to let myself not-quite cry into the scummy water.

There's a clump of feet on the steps to the cabin and I look up, hoping someone has come to rescue me.

But it's a stranger – one, two, three of them – and I lay my head back down across my wrists, wondering whether I have the energy to wash any more when it's all so pointless. The girls go into the cubicles behind me and I tune into their conversation as it bounces across the doors.

"Fucking hell. Can't believe that, can you?"

"We could totally have got backstage if that bouncer hadn't been gay. Flash of the tits, cheeky kiss."

"I did my best!"

"How do you think she got back there?"

"I don't know. Maybe she had a pass?"

There's a flush behind me and one of the girls emerges to wash her hands in the sink next to mine. I feel like telling her that going backstage isn't all it's cracked up to be, but it would be a little weird to crash their conversation.

I stand up and brace my arms on the sink, breathing in and looking at my face in the mirror.

The girl next to me is looking at my reflection and I catch her eye and give her a smile, but she just frowns and glances over her shoulder at her friend who's come out of the far stall. I close my eyes and breathe some more, trying to imagine that the air I'm taking in is making me stronger, that after thirty breaths I will be able to leave the toilet and go find Kaz or Lee or Stu.

I sense someone standing closer than necessary and open my eyes to give whichever girl it is a friendly smile.

She does not smile back. Her mouth and eyes are like three tight little lines slashed in the flesh of her face as she stares at me.

At my arm.

Only then do I realize her friend's on the other side of me, frowning at my reflection.

"Are you the girl who shagged Adam Wexler?"

"Oh my God, is that her?" shouts the third friend, still sorting herself out in the middle cubicle.

"Yes. It's her," I call out with a smile, hoping to lighten the mood a bit. The girls out here resist the lift and just stare at me some more. I turn away from the sink and edge further down the cabin, where there's a towel. The two girls follow my progress, eyes moving like creepy haunted-house paintings.

I decide to ignore them. As soon as their friend comes out, they will leave – and then so will I. All of a sudden I don't feel that being on my own in the toilets is as safe as being out in the crowd.

There's a flush and the friend emerges. She's taller than the other two – pretty in a conventional, healthy, would-be-a-cheerleader-but-only-plays-netball kind of way. Judging by the cut of her vest and the arch of her back, she's the one who tried her best with the allegedly gay bouncer. Like her friends, she shows no shame in staring at me as I carefully dry my hands on the soggy towel looped from the dispenser. It's like being at school.

"What was he like?"

I glance nervously at Did My Best. "Umm … I don't know."

"Wasted, were you?" The first girl. Her eyes are wider now, but her mouth is still an angry little line that she barely opens to talk.

"No." I don't know how to handle this. "Look, I don't want to talk about it."

"So it was shit?"

One of the others cuts in. "I don't believe you. There's no way Adam Wexler would be shit in bed."

"I didn't—"

"So *you* were shit?"

"No, I—" Actually, what do I care? It's not like I'm

trying to sell my sex services to them.

"Did he have a big one?"

"Ha, did you suck it?"

This is making me uncomfortable. "I'm sorry, can I just...?" I do a little duck and point, the way Kaz does when she tries to get past someone.

This move doesn't work, so I try and push past the three of them, but they close up and push me back towards the sink, my spine bumping uncomfortably against the edge.

"... can't believe it..."

"... bet he was thinking of someone else..."

"... not even that pretty..."

"... how did you manage it...?"

"... don't deserve..."

And I snap. I don't break like a twig under too much weight – I explode like a bomb.

"Get the fuck away from me!" I lash out at the nearest one, trying to scare her off, but she dodges and the one next to her squeals at me to watch what I'm doing and palms me right in the chest, so that I'm squashed back between two sinks, my hips knocking painfully on the porcelain. I shove back. "Get away, *get away!*"

But this girl is the perfect picture of health and I am the smallest, the weakest, the least I have ever been and she easily manhandles me away from hurting her, yanking me round, her fingers curled painfully all the way around my arm.

My foot slips on the floor and I fall fast and awkwardly, cracking my head on the rim of the sink. There's an explosion of colours in my eyes and pain rips across my forehead.

"Shit!" I don't know which one it is, because I'm lying on the floor, filthy water soaking into my lovely whimsical unicorn. Through half-closed eyes I see their feet as they hurry out of the door and I think they're going to get help until I hear one of them say, "… not get caught. Shut the door. Everyone'll think it's out of order."

And the door slams shut, leaving me in the dark.

KAZ

The toilets here are relatively deserted – possibly because half the cabins have OUT OF ORDER notices hanging off the doors. I look in all the open ones, ducking to check under the doors in case she's on the floor. Then I ask the attendant who watches people coming and going if she's seen my friend, but the woman just shrugs.

What exactly is the point of having an attendant?

I don't know what to do, so I get my phone out and check for the millionth time whether Ruby's called.

She hasn't.

I decide to call her. I count the rings, willing her to pick up, concentrating so hard that I almost miss the sound of an annoyingly familiar song…

RUBY

Phone's ringing.

Where is it? Not in my hand. I open my eyes to see it lying next to me.

I think I'm reaching out to answer, but actually I'm not moving.

It stops, which is a relief. Don't have to worry about answering it.

My head is killing me.

KAZ

I have to wait for the voicemail to play out before I dial again. This time I hold my phone away from my ear and listen for the ringtone.

There it is.

I look to my left and see a closed cabin, which I walk round, looking for Ruby.

The ringing stops and I wait. Dial again.

I have never been so pleased to hear that stupid song, and it's coming from inside the cabin next to me.

RUBY

I really hope this is just concussion, because there is no way I'm dying.

Just no way.

I want to have sex with Stu again. Lots.

I want to see my stupid brother get on a stupid plane.

I want to have another chance to mock Callum for something and to successfully dead-leg Ed.

I want to tell my parents that I love them, but I'm not resitting my GCSEs. They're enough for what I want to do with my life.

I want to see SkyFires again. They're going to be my new Gold'ntone, without the douchey lead singer. And I want to see the way that non-douchey lead singer looks at my best mate.

Above all, I want to know whatever it is that Stu thinks Kaz needs to tell me. No more secrets. Not between me and Kaz. Not any more.

38 • GROWING UP (FALLING DOWN)

KAZ

The door is stiff and takes a hefty shove for me to open it – the sun from outside spilling out in front of me onto a figure lying on the floor.

"*Ruby…*" Fear and horror and doubt and panic paralyse me for a second until I'm falling onto the floor next to her. There's blood smeared on the sink and a patch of red stickiness on her forehead that's crept down her nose and cheek so it looks as if she's been crying a trail of crimson tears.

That lesson we had in P.E. where we had to practise things like the recovery position and resuscitation was completely useless. I can't remember any of it.

"Don't you *dare* be dead, Ruby Kalinski!" Even saying the word is frightening, but as I say it, I see that she's breathing. My hand is shaking so much that I can't even enter the pin on my phone.

There's a croak on the floor next to me.

"Not dead. Just incredible pain…" Ruby opens one eye and looks up at me. "Hi."

And I burst into tears and press a desperate, grateful (and possibly unwise) kiss on her ear and tell her that I love her.

"You know *I'm* not dying, right?" she says. "Because you and I have some serious catching up to do."

RUBY

Kaz helps me up and I tell her to call Lee – although the opening she uses is not the wisest.

"I found her on the toilet floor. She's bleeding—"

I hear his response from a metre away. "OH MY GOD, IS SHE OK?"

I hold out the hand that's not around Kaz and she gives me her phone. "She's OK, Wee," I say.

"Good, because I'm going to kill you for scaring us like that. Why'd you run off, you loon?"

"I'm not so OK that I can answer that easily." My head is pounding and my thoughts are all jumbled about. "Are you with Stu?"

He isn't. Kaz calls Stu for me and hands me the phone. He answers almost immediately. "Have you found her?"

"She found me," I say with a smile.

There's a deep breath on the other end of the line. "Don't do that to me again, Ruby. Not ever. You understand? No matter what you're running from, can you just wait long enough so I can run with you?"

His words make me want to cry and I'm too all over the place to stop it happening, so I just nod furiously and hand the phone to Kaz to do the talking for me. She tells him that I'm nodding and that I must have done some serious damage to my head because I'm crying. In public. Or rather in a public toilet. And also I am smiling.

Kaz tells me he wants to say something and she holds the phone next to my face.

"I love you, Soho." His words in my ear ease the pain for a second. "I'll see you at the first-aid tent."

As Kaz helps me towards the doorway, I realize I've used too much energy talking to Lee and Stu and when we reach the steps, instead of walking down them, I sit on them. Following my lead, Kaz sits down too.

KAZ

Ruby is paler than I've ever seen her. I would very much like to get her to the first-aid professionals sooner rather than later, but she obviously needs a rest. So obviously that she's now leaning on me, the non-bloody but distinctly damp side of her head resting on my shoulder.

"So Stu says you need to tell me something." She twists her head to look at me. "I'm guessing it's Tom-slash-Lauren related, so spill. In case I bleed out and die anyway."

I'd rather she didn't joke about that kind of thing.

"So you know on Friday?" I say. "When we had a massive fight and you tried to tell me that Tom had a girlfriend and that he was over me?" Ruby does a nod-cum-head loll. "Well, you were right about one of those things."

"I was right about the girlfriend." Then she stops, thinks and adds, "But he was not over you. I totally knew that too, by the way."

Now she tells me. "I found that out the hard way. And I mean that in the most innuendo-ey way possible."

"Shut. Up." Ruby actually sits up and makes me worried that she's upset with me, the way she looks like she's about to shout. "You are *not* telling me you lost your virginity via the medium of innuendo. Nuh-uh. You have to say the words. Repeat after me: *I had sex with Tom*."

"I had sex with Tom."

"That wasn't so hard, was it?" She pats my cheek, and collapses on my shoulder as if perhaps that *was* too hard. Then Ruby adds, "I will beat you up for not telling me about Tom some other time."

"How about me beating you up for not telling me about Adam Wexler?" I tilt my head so she can see I'm grinning, that this is a joke.

"Not sure I'll ever be talking about that one."

I assume she's joking too, because *Adam Wexler*. I can understand why she freaked out about every last person at Remix knowing, but I'm her best friend. I have rights to information like this. "Was he any good?"

"Not for me he wasn't." The way she's talking, the tone of voice she's using doesn't sound like Ruby at all and I realize I misread the truth as a joke. "I couldn't stop thinking that I'd rather be anywhere else than with him."

I stroke her hair away from the cut on her forehead – it's starting to congeal. And there's a rather large lump forming.

"He didn't…?" *How do I even ask this?*

But Ruby and I aren't so far gone that she can't read my mind. "I wanted to. I just really wish I hadn't. Like *really*. Like send someone back in time and *Terminator 2* myself."

"Kill yourself?"

Ruby sighs. "You've never seen *T2*, have you, Kaz?"

I haven't.

"So … was Tom any good, then?" Her voice is back to normal and I decide that I'm never going to ask her about Adam Wexler again. Just because Ruby *can* talk to me about anything, it doesn't mean she has to.

"You have obviously never had sex in a one-man tent," I say.

"No. Just a tour bus." And there's a sigh of laughter in her voice.

"Yours was roomier," I say.

We sit a little longer.

RUBY

"Speaking of rock stars," I say, "anything happen with Sebastian?"

At the mention of his name, my best friend's face blooms into the most beautiful smile. "We kissed. It was nice."

The happiness I can hear in her words makes me want to cry, because there is no one I want to be happy more than Kaz. As she stands, the dress she's wearing floats back in the breeze outlining her body – in the sunlight she seems aglow with Kazness. Strong and sure.

She makes me strong too.

"Come on." Kaz helps me up. "I think we'll go and meet your boyfriend up at the first-aid tent. That head wound is unnerving me."

Boyfriend. Kaz didn't even sound angry when she

called him that.

As I wobble on the steps to the ground, I look down at my vest. "Poor whimsical unicorn. She looks like she just escaped from the abattoir."

"I'll give you my whimsical badger. How about that?" Kaz suggests and I nod – only once, because moving my head is not something that feels all that great.

"Always preferred badgers anyway. Much handier in a fight."

And I slide my hand into Kaz's as we walk back out into the arena. Friendship isn't something that's supposed to be perfect because people aren't perfect. People will lie, they will cheat and they will let you down. Friendship is what picks you up.

You can't pick someone up if they never fall down.

I don't care how many times we fall – one of us will be there to hold the other up.

ACKNOWLEDGEMENTS

Thank you most intensely to Annalie Grainger and Denise Johnstone-Burt. I tried several times to write a sentence that truly expressed why you are so brilliant and I'm sure you know what that sentence should be without me actually writing it – something that sums up the editorial process for *Remix* pretty well, I think. Thank you also to Christian Trimmer whose very sensible thoughts from afar have been invaluable.

Books are a team effort and I am in love with my team mates: Daisy Jellicoe, Jack Noel, Victoria Philpott, Sean Moss ... and everyone else in editorial, design, publicity, marketing, sales, production and rights – just because you aren't named doesn't mean you aren't appreciated. A lot.

Thank you to my amazing agent, Jane Finigan. You pep talk like no other and I continue to be grateful to have you on my side.

This book has changed a lot through the drafting process and I want to thank those who read various incarnations: Laura Hedley, who will always be my litmus test for whether what I've written is utter rubbish; Liz Bankes, whose feedback *without fail* makes me snort-laugh and nod in agreement; Kim Curran, who kindly invested time and thought on the wrong draft (sorry!); and James Dawson, who I caught in time to stop the same thing happening to him. I thank you as readers, but you're pretty awesome as friends too.

Thank you to the book bloggers, not just for your enthusiasm for my book(s), but for books in general. I wish I could thank you all by name, but I would like to give a shout out to Jim Dean, for spreading a particularly happy-making kind of book joy across the Internet.

Speaking of which … thank you, everyone on Twitter, who has suggested a synonym for "having sex", or slang for condoms, made up a stupid (sweary) insult, told me about an unromantic present and above all, thank you A MILLION for all the entertaining, serious, ridiculous and brilliant title suggestions. I'm still a little bit sad we didn't go with the one from @ciclovesbooks: *I Came to this Festival to Forget About My Ex and All I Got Was this Friendship (and Possibly Drugs. But Mainly Friendship)*.

Thank you to the real Kirsten Turner, who won the right for her name (and her left boot) to get written into *Remix*.

Ta muchly to the Masons for coming with me to a festival – Conrad for suggesting we go in the crowd and Kat for introducing me to the phrase "musical omnivore" – and to the friends who accompanied me to gigs in days of yore: Caroline, Katy, Osie, Ruth and Simon.

Thank you, Gemma Cooper, Claire Wilson and Helen Boyle, all of whom help to keep my feet in publishing whilst my head's in another world.

Family, thank you: Mum for what must have been a lot of repetitive phone conversations; Dad for unfailing pride in what I'm doing; Addy for distracting me (not actually very helpful, but never mind); Pragmatic Dan, you can't choose who loves you, which is just as well for me, or I think you'd have chosen someone less erratic, grumpy and messy.

And a kind of pointless (but important) thank you to all the bands who shaped my love of music – there really are few things better than a three-minute-thirty song.

BOY. A GIRL. A BUMP.

TR
O
U
B
L
E

A NOVEL BY
NON PRATT

**"Smart, engaging and hard to put down;
Non Pratt is a YA writer to watch."**
Guardian

Hannah is smart and funny. She's also fifteen
and pregnant. Aaron is the new boy at school.
He doesn't want to attract attention. So why does
Aaron offer to be the pretend dad to Hannah's
unborn baby? Growing up can be trouble but
that's how you find out what really matters.

Ink Slingers
STORIES SET FREE

www.ink-slingers.co.uk